Tess realize choice. She t

"All right," she sai journal. I'll hand it not a moment sooner." sure—and

He didn't answer, and when she tried to withdraw her hand from his much-larger, much-warmer grip, he wouldn't let go, but held on even tighter and tugged her to him, close enough so that his dark gaze was inescapable.

"I could force you to give it to me, you know."

Though shaken, Tess matched his stare without flinching. "I know. But I don't think you would."

His eyes narrowed and she held her breath. "Don't be a fool, Tessa," he warned, his voice hard and low like cold steel wrapped in warm velvet. "You tried to make me into a hero once. It didn't work then and it won't work now."

"Then why should I trust you to help me?"

"Because you have something I want. I'm the same bastard you've hated for almost ten years, Tessa. You'd do well to remember that."

Dear Reader,

What is it about mysterious men that always makes our pulse race? Whether it's the feeling of risk or the excitement of the unknown, dangerous men have always been a part of our fantasies, and now they're a part of Harlequin Intrigue. Throughout 1995, we'll kick off each month with a DANGEROUS MEN title. This month, meet Reed McKenna in *Lethal Lover* by Laura Gordon.

With the Colorado Rockies for inspiration, and her husband and children for moral support, Laura is a full-time writer with a penchant for romantic suspense. She's happiest when creating characters who face danger and discover that the magic of their once-in-a-lifetime love is worth the risk.

With our DANGEROUS MEN promotion, Harlequin Intrigue promises to keep you on the edge of your seat...and the edge of desire.

Sincerely,

Debra Matteucci
Senior Editor and Editorial Coordinator
Harlequin Books
300 East 42nd Street, Sixth Floor
New York, New York 10017

Lethal Lover
Laura Gordon

Harlequin Books

TORONTO • NEW YORK • LONDON
AMSTERDAM • PARIS • SYDNEY • HAMBURG
STOCKHOLM • ATHENS • TOKYO • MILAN
MADRID • WARSAW • BUDAPEST • AUCKLAND

With love,
to my husband, Gordon,
for believing in me and my dreams

ISBN 0-373-22345-5

LETHAL LOVER

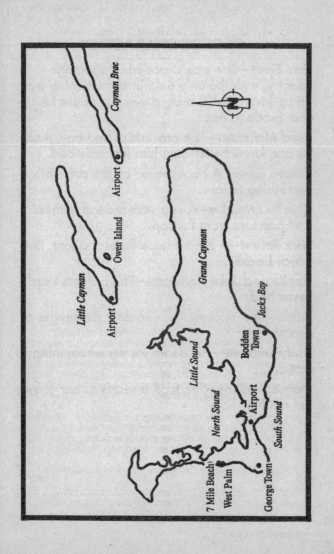

CAST OF CHARACTERS

Tess Elliot—She was stranded in a strange country, with the only help in sight coming from an ex-lover who'd broken every promise he ever made to her.

Reed McKenna—The proverbial bad boy. And no one knew better than him just *how* bad.

Selena Elliot—A bookkeeper on the run, with everything to lose.

Charlie Franklin—A cop with a dead witness and pressure from the top.

Nick Talbot—A by-the-book federal agent, but which book?

Gertie and Jake Patterson—The parents Reed never had.

Paolo—An innocent courier, or a messenger of death?

Andy Dianetti—His death set the whole thing in motion.

Meredith Elliot—She took a secret to her grave, but not her diary.

Chapter One

"Hey, Mac! It's me, Charlie. Pick up the phone! Wake up, Mac. All hell's broke lose out here!"

Reed McKenna swore softly under his breath and reached across the darkness and the pretty blond woman lying next to him to grab the phone.

"I'm here, Charlie," he said, bracing himself for the news he'd been half expecting and half dreading for the past week, ever since Andy Dianetti turned state's witness.

"They got him, Mac. Dianetti's dead."

Reed shifted the cordless receiver to his other ear as the implications of Charlie's grim pronouncement washed over him like tainted water. "When did it happen?" The glowing green digits on his clock radio read 3:29.

"About fifteen minutes ago." The sirens Reed heard wailing in the background were no match for Charlie Franklin's booming baritone. "The firemen found pieces of the car two blocks away. It isn't a pretty sight down here, Mac.''

"It never is." Reed clicked on the reading lamp and fumbled with a pack of gum. He hadn't had a cigarette in almost three weeks, but his craving for that nicotine rush seemed more intense than ever. His jaws ached from chewing gum and his tongue felt raw from sucking Life Savers. "Anyone else hurt?" he asked.

The blonde stirred beside him, but didn't open her eyes.

"The officer who was escorting Dianetti is still alive. Poor bastard. They don't think he'll make it through the night." Charlie hesitated before adding, "I just heard they've found the kid and will be taking her into custody tonight."

A feeling of raw discomfort landed in the pit of Reed's stomach as he stared into the wintry darkness beyond his bedroom window. When he and his companion had come in around midnight it had been snowing; now all he could see when he stared at the glass was his own reflection staring back—dark-haired, dark-eyed, a shadowy silhouette of a man whose heart felt as empty and cold as the night. "And just who was responsible for that brilliant decision?" Reed asked, his tone caustic.

"We have to have the bookkeeper's testimony, Mac. With Andy Dianetti dead, Morrell will walk out of that courtroom free as air if we don't bring her in."

"Then go get her." Reed's suggestion was flatly unsympathetic. "Why drag an innocent kid into the middle of it?"

"If it was that easy," Charlie grumbled, "we wouldn't be calling you and you know it."

Reed scooted to a sitting position, leaning his bare back against the brass headboard. "Just why *did* you call me?" he demanded. "You've got your leverage, use it."

"And take a chance on the media finding out we used the child to blackmail her mother into testifying? That kind of damage would be beyond control. The press would eat us alive!"

Reed could think of worse things. "So what do they want from me? Spell it out, Charlie." He draped his free arm over the woman sleeping beside him. Her skin felt warm and reassuringly alive beneath his hand.

"They want you to bring her in—quietly. No international incidents. Just one civilian to another. Convince her to cooperate, Mac."

Reed ran a hand through his hair. "We've had this conversation before, remember? You told me your guys had it covered."

"Yeah, but that was before Dianetti got himself blown to kingdom come. The stakes just got higher."

"As did my rates."

While Charlie swore, Reed held the phone a few inches from his ear.

"How much?" Charlie asked finally.

"Twice my regular rate," Reed replied, completely refocused on the business at hand. "And since I'll be traveling, my per diem expenses will double, as well."

"Twice!" Charlie exploded. "Think what the hell you're doing to me, Mac! You know what kind of hoops I'll have to jump through to get that kind of money?"

"Like I've told you before—"

"I know, I know. It's not your problem." Charlie sounded exasperated; his ulcer was probably raging again. Too bad, Reed thought. He had no quarrel with Charlie Franklin. The problem lay with his superiors, those white-collared hypocrites on the Hill who demanded results, but kept their own hands lily-white.

He'd worked for them in the past—on both sides of a badge. And he'd work with them now. With luck, this would be the last time.

"Fifteen thousand up front," Reed stated plainly. The kind of answers that could cost a man his life didn't come cheap. "Two hundred thousand on delivery." It was an outrageous demand, but one he knew they'd meet. They wanted the witness, wanted her badly enough to turn Uncle Sam into a kidnapper.

What he didn't know was if two hundred thousand would be enough to give him a fresh start away from the rotten business that he'd become so damn good at. He could only hope so.

"You're crazy, Mac," Charlie grumbled.

"And you're desperate," Reed countered. "Two hundred thousand," he said again. "Cash on delivery. And I want your *leverage* turned over to me, as well."

Charlie gasped. "The kid! You want the kid? You can't be serious."

"I'm completely serious." His sudden and impulsive demand surprised him even more than it had surprised Charlie. It wasn't often that Reed McKenna acted irrationally, but the passion that had risen up and prompted him to do so now was as strong as any force he'd felt in a long, long time. "You heard me, Charlie."

"But what the hell for?"

For Sean, his mind whispered. Reed glanced again at the woman beside him to be sure she was sleeping before he said, "Listen, Charlie, Morrell's bookkeeper has outsmarted your guys for six months, and she's walked a narrow line for a hell of a lot longer than that. She's made half a dozen trips out of the country just this year and she's probably stashed away enough money to support herself into old age. You've admitted yourself that if you had enough to indict her, you wouldn't be calling me. And after what's happened to Dianetti, I need a bargaining chip every bit as much as you do."

"But the kid—you'd really use the kid?"

"And just what the hell were you guys planning to do?"

"Well, we . . ." Charlie sputtered. "That is, they've already picked her up for security reasons . . . to protect her, I guess."

Reed had heard it before, almost the same words, the night they'd taken Sean away from the old man. He hadn't known enough to distrust the system back then and it had cost him his brother. But he knew better now. One dead child was enough for any man to carry on his conscience.

"So you're saying she's safer where she is than with me?"

"Hell, yes!"

"Can you guarantee that, Charlie?"

The older man's sigh was weary. "All right, Mac, I admit I don't know how it will all work out, but I do know these people are set up for kids. They've got homes, you know?"

He knew.

"And people, experts who know how to deal with things like this. Come on, Mac. Forget the kid, will ya? She'll be safe."

"Tell that to Dianetti, you son of a bitch," Reed growled, slamming the phone down, half choking on the unexpected surge of anger Charlie's indifference had provoked.

The phone rang again almost immediately. Reed grabbed it on the second ring, but didn't bother to say hello.

"It's gonna take time," Charlie's tone seemed resigned. "It's a lot of money and getting temporary custody of the kid transferred to you won't be easy."

Reed wasn't in the mood for bureaucratic excuses. "One hour," he said simply.

"One hour!" the older man exploded. "Damn it, man! It would take a presidential order to get things moving that fast."

"Then I suggest you call him," Reed replied, reminding himself that time was something he didn't have to waste.

He'd begun researching the situation a week ago, just in case he was called. Pulling in every marker owed him, he'd been able to learn where the bookkeeper was headed; it was invaluable information that would at least assure him a head start.

But it was a fragile lead at best. With Dianetti out of the picture, Reed knew he'd be only one of many stalking Edward Morrell's elusive bookkeeper. True, Reed had had an edge in tracking her, a personal connection he hoped to hell Morrell would never discover. Nevertheless, if he'd been able to discover her plans in less than a week, it wouldn't take the other side much longer.

Even now he felt the clock pushing him. In the last five minutes, getting the bookkeeper's kid safely out of the country had suddenly become Reed's top priority. Then he'd worry about finding the bookkeeper, convincing her to come back to the States and keeping her alive to testify.

And as if that wasn't enough, there in the background was Tess. How did life get so tangled? Thoughts of Tess, of the fire storm into which she was unwittingly walking made his pulse race as if a time bomb were already ticking.

"You have my terms," he reminded Charlie. "One hour," he muttered again into the receiver and imagined the sweat beading on the older man's forehead.

"You're one cold S.O.B., anybody ever tell you that, Mac?"

Reed allowed himself a grim smile. "Yeah, once or twice." He stabbed the disconnect button and looked up to see the blonde's pale blue eyes open and staring up at him. "Time to go home, Cinderella," he said as he swung his legs over the side of the bed and stood up.

"But—"

"No buts, babe. I have work to do." He grabbed his jeans and pulled them on, wondering how long it would take him to put together a traveling nursery. *The kid.* He'd demanded temporary custody of the kid. He almost couldn't believe it himself.

"Work?" the blonde grumbled as she sat up and reached for her scattered clothes. "What kind of job calls you out in the middle of the night?"

Reed ignored her question; to explain himself to a woman he'd known less than five hours seemed pointless.

After she'd called for a taxi, she sat down on the bed and tugged on her knee-high boots. Reed grabbed his duffel bag out of the closet and proceeded to pack.

"Hey, you're leaving town, aren't you?"

"It looks that way." Funny, Reed thought, she hadn't seemed the talkative type a few hours ago.

"Will I see you again when you get back? Will you call me?" Her voice was smoky and her breath smelled faintly of the scotch they'd both consumed in ample quantities at the bar where they'd met earlier in the evening.

"Maybe."

"Well, you've got my number. Maybe I'll see you at Duffy's again. A bunch of us usually hang out there on Fridays after work."

Reed merely smiled and nodded as he finished packing. When he reached past her to withdraw the .38 semiautomatic he kept taped behind the headboard, her eyes widened.

She watched as Reed slipped it into an interior pocket of his favorite leather jacket. Newly impressed by the dangerous-looking man before her, she asked, "So tell me, Mac, where are you going in the middle of the night in such a hurry?"

Unbidden, a voice from his past came back to answer. "I'm headed to hell, babe," he said. "Like my old man always said, 'straight to hell on a fast train.'"

And if Edward Morrell didn't get to him first, Reed told himself, Tess Elliot would be only too happy to punch his ticket.

Chapter Two

The waiter who showed Tess and Selena Elliot across the open-air dining room was a tall, handsome young man with a perfect tan and light brown hair naturally streaked by the sun. Taking in his all-American looks, Tess would have thought him more at home in Southern California than Grand Cayman.

But when he spoke, his English was seasoned with that unique, melodic Caribbean accent that Tess found charming, and she realized that he must be a native. His uniform was the loose-fitting, multicolored shirt and white canvas trousers that all the West Palm staff members wore.

"Well, what do you think of paradise so far?" Selena asked. "Aren't you glad you came?" Her cousin's blue eyes, so similar in hue and shape to Tess's own, were bright as she sat down in the chair the waiter pulled out for her.

"You were right, Selena, everything here is sheer heaven." Tess leaned back in her chair and inhaled the pure ocean air and scanned the magnificent view from their balcony table. "Everything is exactly as you said it would be."

Selena beamed. "Rum punch for both of us. West Palm has the best rum punch on the island," she informed Tess when their waiter had left.

Tess rolled her eyes and smiled. "Well, if it packs the same wallop as the two I had on the plane, I think we'd better order dinner soon."

"Oh, come on, chicken," Selena teased. "It's only a little past three. Besides, when you're on vacation it's always cocktail hour!" Her smile was mischievous. "Let yourself go, Tess. Or, as they say on the island, don't worry, be happy!"

Tess laughed and took another deep breath of the naturally perfumed air as she wondered how anyone could help but relax when immersed in such an idyllic environment. The scene beyond the balcony was a living postcard of sugar white sands and sparkling, sapphire water. Overhead was an endless expanse of cloudless blue. In the distance, small fishing boats drifted and bobbed aimlessly on the shimmering sea.

A dozen tourists basked in the afternoon sun on folding chairs and bright beach towels at the water's edge. Laughter from a group of bikini-clad teenagers playing volleyball mingled with the rhythmic beat of Caribbean music drifting from the bar at the opposite end of the dining room.

"Ah, here we are," Selena exclaimed, and Tess turned to see their waiter returning with two huge glasses frosted and filled to the rim with the same sparkling, red concoction that the Cayman Airlines flight attendants had served nonstop during the hour-and-a-half flight from Miami.

The waiter offered menus, but Selena waved them away. "We'll order later. Right now, we're celebrating."

Tess felt like giggling; Selena's expansive mood was contagious. "Selena, I never knew you to be...well, so much fun. If this is a preview of things to come, this trip will be one I won't soon forget."

Selena arched one thin, dark brown brow and leaned across the table, fixing her gaze on her younger cousin. "Okay, so maybe the next time I ask you to join me on vacation, you won't be so hard to convince?"

"I was a bit difficult, wasn't I?" Tess admitted sheepishly. To say that she'd been stunned when Selena had first mentioned their joint excursion to Grand Cayman, would have been an understatement. Flabbergasted was a more apt description of how she'd reacted when Selena had called a month ago with the idea of a holiday for the two of them.

Initially, Tess had refused her cousin's offer outright. The small bookstore she owned and managed in Evergreen, Colorado was in its infancy; every penny that came in was still being turned back into the business it had taken Tess two years to launch.

But when Selena had explained that she'd won the trip as a reward from her company and that the prize entitled her to bring a guest, Tess had reconsidered.

"It's a pathetic state of affairs for a red-blooded woman of thirty-two, but I have to admit it—I have no *significant other,*" Selena had quipped. "Seriously, I think this trip would do us both good. Mom and Dad would have been so pleased to see us off together on a romp." At the mention of her recently deceased aunt and uncle, Tess had begun to cave in.

When Selena tapped her hand, Tess started. "Earth to Tess, come in, cousin," she teased. "All right. Now that I have your attention, I want to propose a toast. To family."

Tess raised her glass to Selena's. "To Phil and Marjorie."

Selena nodded, her bright expression dimming. "Yes, to my parents. They always wanted us to be friends, especially Mom. Remember?"

Tess *did* remember, and not without a twinge of regret. "I guess we let them down, didn't we?"

"It wasn't your fault," Selena admitted. "I was the brat who couldn't share. Never could."

"Selena, don't—"

"No, no, I admit it." Her gaze fell away from Tess's and focused on the glass she held with both hands. "I can still remember the night my parents called me at school to tell me what had happened to your mom and dad and Meredith. . . . Mom could hardly talk she was so devastated. She and her sister had been best friends. And I was devastated, as well. But mainly because I knew it meant you'd be coming to live with us." Selena's expression was distant for a moment. "Frankly, I hated you then," she admitted and lifted her glass to drink deeply.

Selena's frank admission caused Tess to wince, but more painful by far was the memory of the accident that had claimed her family.

"Selena, please . . . let's don't go on with this."

"You were so pretty, so sweet and so, oh, I don't know—so everything I wasn't. Good grades, a natural athlete, popular. I was the struggling business major with the student loan. You were the bright-eyed freshman, the one with the full scholarship. At the time, C.U. didn't seem big enough for the two of us."

Tess reached across the table and covered Selena's hand with her own. "Please stop, Selena. What's past is past." *A past too painful to look back at,* Tess finished to herself.

"You know, except for funerals, we've hardly seen each other in the last six years. And now, here I go spoiling our vacation by behaving as though we're attending another one."

Tess's mouth went dry and she reached for her drink, thinking that the festive mood that had bubbled between them just a few minutes ago had fallen as flat as the rum punch.

"You know, I never realized just how much my family meant to me until I lost my own parents," Selena admitted.

Tess nodded, remembering how valiantly Aunt Marjorie had battled the unrelenting illness that had finally claimed her life four years ago. Then a year later Uncle Phil had been snatched from them by an unexpected and fatal heart attack.

"I know how you're feeling," Tess said sympathetically. "Even after all this time, I still miss my parents and my sister."

"Sometimes it's just so difficult." Selena gazed past Tess wistfully.

During the silence that stretched between them, Tess thought about her parents and Meredith and the terrible call that had come in the middle of the night. She'd been nineteen, a year out of high school, ready for college after taking a year out to work at a bookstore. She'd been poised to embark on a life that had seemed nearly perfect—too perfect, she reminded herself. Then suddenly the people she'd loved most in the world were gone. Mom. Dad. Meredith. And even Reed.

Reed McKenna, her first real love, her first lover. He'd walked out on her mere days before she'd lost her family in the accident. Then she'd lost him all over again when she stumbled over her sister's diary. Eight long years, and the loss and betrayal still hurt.

"Oh, come on," Selena prodded, dragging Tess from the depths of her dark memories. "Enough of this gloom and doom. We're supposed to be on vacation, remember? Two young women, footloose and fancy-free for two whole weeks on an island paradise."

Tess summoned her best face. "That's us." She lifted her glass again. "To Selena and Tess, look out Grand Cayman!" *And to forgiving and forgetting,* she added to herself. If it was time for a new beginning with her only living relative, surely it was time to let go of the painful past.

"To family." Selena's smile seemed as forced as Tess's.

They touched glasses, but before they could drink, Tess noticed their waiter approaching again. "Perhaps we should look at the menu now," she suggested.

"Excuse me," the waiter said. "But there is a phone call in the lobby for Miss Elliot."

"For me?" the cousins asked simultaneously, and then looked at each other and laughed.

"I doubt it could be for me," Tess said. "My manager has strict instructions that unless the store burns down with the insurance policy inside, I'm not to be disturbed."

Selena groaned and pushed back her chair.

"Wait a minute, I bet it's the rental-car company," Tess suggested, recalling the mix-up at the airport that had caused an hour's delay getting a car. "I can go talk to them if you'd like." But when she started to get up, Selena stopped her.

"No, you stay put," she insisted. "It's probably my office. They don't know the meaning of the word *vacation*. Order an appetizer, some shrimp or something. I won't be a minute." Before Tess could say more, Selena was hurrying away from the table.

As she watched her cousin leave, she noticed a man at the bar across the room watching her, as well. Tess couldn't blame him. Selena was an attractive woman.

Like Tess, Selena was tall—almost five nine—and trim. It occurred to Tess as she watched her cousin disappear into the lobby that she'd never seen Selena looking more fit. She'd lost at least ten pounds, Tess figured, remembering how grief could take a toll.

Today, dressed in a bright pink sundress and jaunty straw hat, Selena looked pretty as a picture. She'd turned heads from the moment they'd stepped off the plane in Georgetown. Like Tess, Selena wore her hair past her shoulders. But while Tess's was straight and blunt cut, Selena wore springy curls and she'd lightened the dark brown that they'd both inherited from their mothers' side of the family to an attractive, sun-kissed, ash blond.

Selena was not only attractive, but an independent and successful businesswoman. Tess wasn't exactly sure just what kind of business Selena was engaged in, but whatever it was, her cousin had to be doing well, as evidenced by this trip.

Beautiful, successful, confident—all those adjectives could rightly be used to describe her only cousin, Tess told herself. Surely the old jealousy that had kept Selena from allowing a relationship to bloom between them could at last be put to rest.

"Well, here's to you, Selena," Tess murmured as she brought her glass to her lips again and took another sip. "To the future."

THE PERSISTENCE of the breakers pounding the rocks below the balcony restaurant had nothing on the unrelenting memories pummeling Reed McKenna as he sat transfixed, watching Tess Elliot where she sat at her table across the room.

She was even more beautiful than the indelible image he carried in his memory. If she had changed at all, it was only for the better. She was still startlingly attractive. Her smile was still a cover girl's. Her hair still long, thick and glossy brown. Even from this distance, he could tell that her olive skin still glowed with good health, as though she'd just stepped off one of her beloved Colorado mountain trails.

When she'd walked in, wearing the gauzy yellow sundress, he couldn't help noticing that her long legs were still slim and well toned, and that she still moved like a thoroughbred.

When she'd laughed, the sound had floated to him on a breeze and sparked what few memories hadn't already been stirred to life by the sudden sight of her. *Tess,* his mind whispered, *what kind of fool would ever let you go?*

"Can I get you another beer, sir?" the bartender asked, interrupting Reed's musings.

He nodded, resisting the temptation to ask the bartender to bring him a pack of Camels.

Out of the corner of his eye, Reed saw the waiter deliver a message to Selena Elliot. When she stood up and walked out of the dining room, Reed hoped that Tess wouldn't follow.

Selena left the dining room alone, and Reed decided with grim satisfaction that perhaps this wasn't going to be as difficult as he'd first thought. Maybe he wouldn't have to inflict himself on Tess after all.

That *was* the way he wanted it, wasn't it? Of course, he reminded himself. The memories he'd harbored, the fantasies he'd spun about his young love, were just that: fantasies and nothing more.

But despite that blunt realization, before he left the bar, he couldn't resist a last look over his shoulder at the woman who'd once held his young heart, before it had turned cold. And captured his imagination, before it had become so jaded.

Her eyes met his for barely a second and he foolishly held his breath, wondering if she recognized him.

When it appeared she hadn't, a strange mix of disappointment and relief settled heavily in his chest.

WHEN THE SHIMMERING crystal bowl of chilled shrimp arrived, Tess began to wonder what was keeping Selena. After five minutes more, she beckoned their waiter. "Excuse me, but could you direct me to the phone where my cousin took her phone call?"

"Of course," the young man agreed. "Right this way."

The bar was beginning to fill and the waiter and Tess had to weave their way past a group gathered around a table where a lively game of dominoes was in progress.

Once in the lobby, the young man pointed to a bank of courtesy phones on the wall. From where she stood, Tess could already see that Selena was not in the lobby.

"Perhaps she had the call transferred to our room," Tess suggested. "I think I'll go check. If she comes back before I do, will you tell her where I've gone?"

The waiter smiled and nodded.

Crossing the lobby quickly, Tess emerged onto the sidewalk outside the main building that led to the individual guest rooms. A profusion of tropical plants, bay vines and spider lilies, lined the meandering walk that led to three separate buildings. The music and laughter coming from the beach faded as she made her way up the open stairway to the fourth floor of the first building.

At their room, Tess unlocked the door and stepped inside. The large, airy room was empty and Tess saw no obvious sign to suggest that Selena had returned since the two of them had gone down to the dining room for dinner.

With a nagging and growing sense of anxiety, Tess walked back to the lobby, crossed the dining room and sat down at their table alone. She beckoned to the first waiter that passed, but when the young man turned around, she realized he wasn't the same waiter who'd helped them earlier. "Excuse me, but did the other lady who was sitting here return while I was gone?"

The young man's expression was blank. "I haven't seen anyone, ma'am, not since I came on duty a few minutes ago. Can I bring you something to drink, or a menu?"

Tess shook her head. "No thanks," she muttered distractedly, looking past him, searching the room for Selena. After picking unenthusiastically at the shrimp and sipping the lukewarm punch for ten long minutes, Tess decided to check the lobby again.

Still, there was no sign of Selena. The ladies' room was Tess's next stop, but her cousin was not to be found there, either.

Wandering back into the lobby, Tess began to feel stronger stirrings of concern. A noisy group of tourists jostled off a tour bus, into the lobby and crowded around the front desk. Tess tried in vain to pick out her cousin's face among the group.

A tall, sandy-haired man in a brightly printed floral shirt and baggy white shorts caught Tess's eye when she realized he was staring at her. But when she made eye contact, he looked away. An uneasy feeling lifted the hair at the nape of her neck, but she dismissed the strange reaction and searched the lobby again for Selena.

Where could she have gone? Tess wondered, walking back to the entrance to the dining room to stand helplessly staring across the room at their empty balcony table as gnawing apprehension bloomed into genuine concern.

"May I help you, miss?" A cocktail waitress in a short, floral wrap skirt and yellow halter top greeted Tess when she stepped into the crowded bar.

"I'm looking for someone...." Tess murmured distractedly, her eyes scanning the crowd. "A woman, about my height, in a pink sundress and a big hat. Have you seen her?"

The young woman attendant's eyes followed Tess's around the room. "No, I don't remember seeing anyone like that. But then, the place has been filling up fast since the last group of dive boats came in," she explained in perfect, West Indies English. "If I see her, I will be sure to tell her that you're looking for her."

Tess thanked the young woman and moved back into the lobby, completely at a loss as to what to do next, or how to explain her cousin's strange disappearance. As she wandered toward the main door and the circle drive in front of the hotel, a limousine slid to a stop outside and reminded her of the problem with the rental car.

Heartened to have a course of action, Tess walked briskly to the nearest courtesy phone and dialed the number for the rental-car company.

After a short and disjointed explanation to the clerk on the other end of the line, Tess gave up, thanked the woman for her help—which had, in fact, been no help at all—and hung up, feeling even more exasperated. If the call that had pulled Selena away from their table had come from the rental-car company, the person to whom Tess had spoken knew nothing about the matter.

When Tess glanced at the large clock on the wall behind the registration desk, she saw that it was nearly four-thirty. Selena had left their table almost forty-five minutes ago. *Where was she?*

Feeling someone's eyes on her, Tess spun around, hoping to see Selena, only to find the man in the gaudy shirt staring at her again. She glared at the tourist and the man actually smiled, causing Tess to feel even more peevish as she pushed her way to the front desk.

After leaving a message for Selena, Tess left the lobby quickly with the eerie feeling that gaudy-shirt-man's eyes were still on her back.

Once inside their room again, Tess set her mind to the task of unpacking and tried to tell herself that any moment Selena would come bursting through the door, smiling and apologetic with a breathless explanation for her strange disappearance. But soon another fifteen minutes had ticked by, and Selena hadn't returned.

After her things were put away, Tess paced out onto the balcony and scanned the beach and squinted to see as far as she could in each direction.

Tess figured Selena's bright pink dress and big floppy hat would have been easy to spot if she had been among the people wandering along the beach. But there was no pink dress. No floppy hat. No Selena. Something was dreadfully wrong, she was nearly certain.

When the phone finally rang, it startled her. Her heart pounded and she banged her knee on the nightstand hurrying back inside. The receiver was halfway to her ear when someone knocked on the door. "Just a minute," she called out.

"Hello," she answered hopefully into the receiver. "Hold on!" she shouted to the persistent knocker on the other side of the door. "Hello!" she said again into the phone.

"Miss Elliot, this is Guy from Premium Car Rental. I understand you're having a problem with your car?"

"No, no, there's nothing wrong with the car!" Tess felt her heart sink. "Yes, I did call earlier, but—" The knocking grew louder.

"Hang on a minute," she told the car-rental clerk, dropping the phone on the bed and hurrying across the room to open the door.

Reaching for the door, Tess just knew it would be Selena's pretty face she'd see on the other side.

She jerked the door open and every teasing word she'd prepared to fling at her cousin for losing her keys or forgetting the time or whatever froze on Tess's lips as she stood staring and speechless at Reed McKenna, as tall, dark and startlingly handsome as ever, standing in her doorway.

With just one look, Tess knew her life was about to change forever.

Chapter Three

There were no words to express her shock; only his name emerged. "Reed?" It came out a whisper.

"Hello, Tess."

Her heart was a jackhammer in her chest. "Wh-what—"

"What am I doing here?" he finished the question as he strode past her into the room. "I guess I could ask you the same thing, couldn't I, Tess? Close the door, why don't you?"

Numbly, she followed his instructions, the jolt of seeing Reed again, here in Grand Cayman, in her hotel room, had completely dumbfounded her. Rational thought told her he hadn't materialized simply by her early thoughts of him, but then again, there was nothing rational about the way her heart raced at the sight of him.

"Nice," he noted as he stepped deeper into the room, picked up the phone that was still lying on the bed and dropped it back onto its base.

Still thunderstruck by his presence, Tess could only stand and stare as he crossed to the balcony and peered outside. Her whole body seemed to be trembling and she couldn't stop her thoughts from taking a jet-propelled trip back in time.

He'd been the town's bad boy, the kind of young man mothers warned their daughters about while secretly harboring fantasies of their own involving the darkly handsome, street-smart kid from the proverbial wrong side of the tracks. Quick-witted, handsome, cocky—all these were traits Reed McKenna possessed in abundance, traits that combined to give him that hypnotic magnetism that women couldn't resist and men couldn't help but admire.

Seeing him now, dressed in softly faded jeans and a white polo shirt and looking twice as handsome and even sexier, Tess couldn't help remembering the way he'd stirred her passions. Seeing his faint blue-black beard shadow enhancing his rugged maleness, and his dark brown eyes as intensely seductive and compelling as ever, Tess felt the old familiar attraction drawing her to him again.

Get hold of yourself. You're a grown woman, not some lovesick teenager! But even as that inner voice scolded, the years melted away and the sweat rose on her palms. *Damn you, Reed McKenna! Damn your lean body and your thick, black hair and the wicked brown eyes that always seemed to be looking right into my very soul.* And damn that smile of his that curled his perfect lips and drove dimples into his lean, tanned checks.

He turned and sent his smoky gaze sliding leisurely up and down the length of her. "Surprised to see me?" Another smile, and appealing lines winged out from the corners of his eyes.

"Surprised? Believe me, surprised doesn't even come close. What *are* you doing here?" she asked him again.

"So that's all you can say? Not even 'how's it going, Reed?' or 'Gee, but it's damn good to see you after all this time'?"

It wasn't damn *good* to see him, it was damn disturbing and damn perplexing, exasperating, wonderful and a host of other jumbled and conflicting emotions, all of which Tess despised.

She ran a hand carelessly through her hair, scrambling to collect her wits and raise her guard. "I see you haven't changed. Still playing word games, still incapable of giving a straight answer."

His look was one of practiced innocence that she recognized and responded to, despite herself. "Well, you know what they say about teaching old dogs new tricks," he drawled.

She would not be drawn in, she promised herself, by the patented McKenna charm. "The last I heard you were some kind of federal cop in D.C.," she said to change the subject.

His thick lashes dipped lazily. "And the last I heard you were back home running some kind of specialty bookstore."

"Mysteries, Ltd.," she informed him tersely, realizing too late that he'd deftly avoided answering her question by shifting the focus back on her. Just like the old Reed, she told herself, always a jump ahead of everyone. Always setting the rules.

"Mysteries, huh? Well, what do you know," his voice held a note of mild indifference as his gaze swept the room before he sauntered toward the bathroom, opened the door and glanced in.

Tess was flabbergasted by his actions and inflamed by his arrogance. "Excuse me, but just what the hell are you doing?" she demanded, coming up behind him with her hands on her hips. He was giving the bathroom such intense scrutiny that she figured if the shower curtain had been drawn he'd have pushed it open to search the tub as well.

He turned away from the bathroom and glanced at the two queen-size beds separated by a standard hotel nightstand. "Nice room."

"You said that before."

His gaze wandered back to her and a bemused grin tugged at his mouth, making her feel suddenly exposed in the sundress that had seemed perfectly appropriate until now. "You always were the direct one, weren't you, Tessa?"

She started at the sound of the pet name no one had called her in almost ten years. "You're still impossible."

"And you're still angry."

"Angry?" she muttered, detesting the way his mere presence had toppled her emotional equilibrium. "Now, what would give you that impression, McKenna? Let's see—" Desperate for distance, she turned her back to him and stalked to the other side of the room. "Someone I haven't laid eyes on in, what? Almost five years—" When she turned around to face him again, he had dropped down into the wicker chair that sat beside the sliding glass doors.

"Four and a half years, at the airport in Denver," he supplied. "You were on your way to see a sick relative."

"Am I supposed to be impressed that you remembered?"

He shrugged, but his expression told her he knew she was secretly pleased. Inside she seethed, hating him for knowing her so well and despising the fact that he could still read her emotions so effortlessly.

"Where was I?" she said. "Ah, yes, we were trying to figure out why I should be angry with you for waltzing in without an iota of an explanation. And let's not forget the part about the wedding you conveniently forgot to attend. When was that, Reed, since you're the one who's so good at remembering?"

His smile had disappeared and his mouth was set in a tight line as he studied her.

"I see you can't remember. Well, let me refresh your memory. It was eight years ago, Reed. June 15th to be exact. Three days before—" Her voice broke and she lowered her eyes to avoid looking at the face that would, if she stared at it long enough, eventually undo her.

He stood and stared out at the beach. "I was sorry to hear about your parents, Tess."

"I lost my sister, as well," she reminded him pointedly. Although she was dry-eyed, her heart ached.

"I know," he said quietly. "And I'm sorry. Meredith was a good kid."

Tess felt her heart harden at the sound of her sister's name coming from his lips. How dare he? And how foolish was she to stand here jousting with the man who'd single-handedly destroyed her girlhood innocence and shattered her dreams?

Crossing the room purposefully, she jerked open the door and stood with one hand planted on each hip. "Angry? No, Reed, I'm not angry. But I *am* a lot wiser than that fawning nineteen-year-old you left standing at he altar." Her diatribe left her breathless and the flood of heat that rose to her cheeks left her feeling weak. "I don't know why you're here, Reed, but I'm vacationing, and I know I'll enjoy myself a whole lot more if I just throw you out and pretend this little meeting never occurred. Now, if you'll excuse me," she finished with a flourish, "I'd appreciate it if you got the hell out of my room and stayed the hell out of the rest of my life!"

He stood staring at her for a long tense moment before he started toward the door. Tess held her breath, hardly daring to believe that he'd actually leave without a fight. The old Reed would never have backed down so easily.

And neither would the new Reed, it seemed, for when he was directly in front of her, he surprised her by taking her hand and pulling her out of the doorway, before pushing the door closed and leaning against it with his arms crossed over his broad chest.

"Where's Selena?" he asked, all pretense of word games abruptly ended.

"Selena?" Tess asked, unable to conceal her shock.

He nodded. "You asked me what I was looking for. Well, I was looking for your cousin, Selena Elliot."

Tess blinked. To her knowledge her cousin and her ex-fiancé had never met. When Selena was growing up, she and her parents had lived in Denver, while Tess and Reed had grown up in the small mountain town of Evergreen some thirty miles west. She'd become involved with Reed McKenna her senior year and she had been working the year before starting college when he'd broken their engagement by suddenly, and without telling her, enlisting in the army. It was only later, when she'd inadvertently discovered his betrayal, that

Tess had finally learned the real reason Reed had left town.

"Where is she?" he asked, jolting Tess back to the present.

"Why do you want to know?" she shot back defensively. "What connection do you have to Selena?"

"I don't have any connection, not personally, anyway. I'm only here to take her back to the States. If you care about your cousin, you'll tell me where she is and stay out of the way so I can do my job."

"Your job?" Tess realized she was staring at him like an idiot, but the things he'd just said made no sense. "Then you *are* a cop."

He didn't answer.

"And you're here to arrest Selena? This is unbelievable! What has she done, what's this all about?" If Selena was in some kind of trouble, wouldn't she have mentioned it? Or at least canceled this trip?

Reed didn't answer any of her questions, but his dark-eyed stare continued to bore through her.

"Listen, Reed, whatever you want with my cousin, I know you can't force her to go anywhere without some kind of warrant or subpoena."

"I'm not here to arrest her," he admitted.

Well, at least he'd given her that much. But Tess wasn't satisfied. All her instincts warned that Reed was concealing far more than he'd revealed.

"All right, so you don't have a warrant, then why are you looking for her and why should she go anywhere with you?"

His eyes flashed his irritation at being questioned. "Because the U.S. government has requested the honor of her presence at a trial."

"A trial," she repeated numbly, feeling slightly light-headed. "What kind of trial? Whose trial? I—I don't understand. What's going on and what has my cousin got to do with it?"

"It's a long story," he said as he walked across the room to the balcony again. She followed him and watched as his eyes scanned the beach below.

Finally he returned his attention to Tess's question. "You really don't know anything about all this, do you? She hasn't told you?"

"Told me what?" Tess demanded, her patience stretched almost to snapping. "What don't I know?"

He stood for another long moment without answering, without even looking at her. Exasperated, she reached for his arm, but the minute her fingers made contact with the warm, tanned flesh her heart jumped, and she knew she'd made a mistake. Immediately she pulled her hand back, feeling inexplicably singed.

"Reed, please. Tell me what this is all about. If my cousin is in some kind of trouble, I have a right to know." And if this is just a bad dream, Tess told herself, she wished to hell someone would wake her!

"Selena is in trouble," he conceded finally, taking her elbow and ushering her inside the room with him. "She works for a man who's been indicted on federal charges."

Tess sat down woodenly on the edge of the bed. "What kind of charges?"

"Racketeering, money laundering and murder, just to name a few."

Tess felt exactly as she had as a child the time she'd fallen from the monkey bars on the playground and had the wind knocked out of her. "I don't believe it," she gasped.

"Believe it," he said and pulled the bow-shaped wicker chair around to face her before he sat down. "Selena worked as a bookkeeper for Edward Morrell. She was a key figure in his organization."

Tess could only sit and stare at him, her mind whirling as she tried to make sense of something that made no sense at all.

"Look, I can see how hearing all of this has shocked you, and it's obvious to me that you know nothing about your cousin's involvement." He rose and put the chair back in its place before he added, "I'd like to help you put it all together, but I haven't got time to explain. And I'm not sure it's wise to tell you any more than I already have. But I need to know where she is, Tess," he said, coming back to the bed to stand over her. "I need to find her and get her out of Grand Cayman tonight."

The unthinkable occurred to Tess in a flash of frightening insight and she rose quickly, oblivious to the precious space that she'd closed between them and the fact that she'd planted her hands on his chest. "Reed, are you trying to tell me that Selena might be in some kind of danger?"

He glanced down at her hands resting on his chest, before his eyes met hers again. "Just tell me where she is, Tess, if you know."

His dark eyes grew even darker and suddenly every protective instinct went off in a series of screaming alarms inside Tess's mind. She nearly stumbled, side-stepping away from him. "I won't tell you anything until you tell me what this is all about."

"Where is she, Tess?" he demanded, his voice hard-edged and impatient.

"I don't know," she insisted. "And even if I did, I wouldn't tell you. Did you seriously imagine I'd blindly turn my cousin over to you without talking to her first?"

"I'd hoped you would be reasonable."

"Reasonable or gullible?"

She watched a muscle clench at his jaw and for an uneasy moment she wondered if Selena might be running from him. "You always were too damn stubborn for your own good," he muttered as he turned and headed for the door.

She was on his heels. "And just when did what's good for me ever interest you, McKenna?"

His eyes blazed and Tess felt the fire of his anger, but she refused to be cowed, despite his seething temper and his obvious strength advantage—an advantage that by the looks of his lean, hard body was considerable.

"All right," he relented finally, breaking their staring match. Tess felt a long-overdue twinge of satisfaction. "I guess you have a right to know the circumstances. But when I've finished telling you, your stay in Grand Cayman will be over. You'll have to pack your bags and fly back to the States on the next available flight."

She rankled at his direct order. "But—"

"No argument," he said sharply. "From now on you do as I say, Tessa, as though your life depended on it."

And from the grim expression on his face, Tess believed that it just might.

ONE FLOOR BELOW Tess Elliot's room, a naked toddler sitting in a tub of warm water squealed with delight at the spray of water she raised every time she slapped a small, pink, plastic elephant and sent it bobbing. "Doggy, doggy, doggy," she chanted and giggled and splashed.

The middle-aged woman bent over the tub and laughed and pulled her saturated cotton blouse away from her skin. "Whatever you say, Sweetie."

"Doggy!" the child responded gleefully, her small pink mouth curled into a delighted grin that revealed four small, shining, front teeth—two on top, two on the bottom.

"Are you trying to drown the kid, Gertie?" a male voice teased from the bathroom door.

"You go on and mind your own business, Jake. Me and little Miss Crissy is having us a great time."

Jake stuck his bald head in the doorway, and enjoyed the sight of his wife of forty-plus years sitting on the floor, seemingly oblivious to the puddle of water around her or the blouse that stuck to her like a second skin.

"Who's giving who the bath?" he asked mischievously.

Gertie shook her head and rolled her eyes. "Listen to him, will you, Crissy? The man's a certified comic, ain't he?"

The little girl with the big blue eyes and honey gold ringlets tossed her head and giggled at a joke she couldn't possibly understand. Gertie opened a towel and lifted Crissy out of the tub.

The sight of the child in Gertie's arms caused Jake's heart to constrict. The poor little thing had no idea she was being used as a pawn in a game where the rules were being made up as they went along.

"Gertie," Jake said, his voice low as he edged over to the toilet and sat down on the lid, "do you think we did right by agreeing to do this?"

Gertie wrapped the plush white towel snugly around the child's chubby middle and swept Crissy into her arms. "Of course we did the right thing. What's the matter with you, old man?" When the child reached for her glasses, Gertie had to arch her neck to save them. "Besides, how could we have turned him down? After all he's done for us, and never once asked for anything in return."

Jake hung his head. "You're right, hon. It's just that—"

"It's just nothing," Gertie cut him off. "Reed McKenna asked us to take care of this little gal for a few days and that's what we're going to do."

"You're right, Gert," Jake said as he stood up and followed her into the bedroom. "I just hope he knows what he's doing. It don't seem right for a child to be separated from her—"

Gertie interrupted him again. "Don't say it," she snapped, turning on him, "or else you'll get her to crying all over again."

Jake sighed and paced to the window to look out at the beach. "Reckon we could take her outside to play when she wakes up? The little thing is so pale. She needs some fresh air." And so did Jake.

"Probably. Now, go take a walk, will you? You're making me and the baby nervous with all your pacing."

Jake Patterson started for the door. "Bring us back some sandwiches and chips," his wife called after him.

"And remember to get a carton of milk and some fruit for Crissy and a couple of them punch drinks for us. We'll save them for later, and after this little dolly goes to bed, we'll sit out on the balcony and have us a picnic."

Jake forced a smile and walked out of his third-floor hotel room, making sure the door closed and locked behind him.

"I DON'T BELIEVE YOU!" Tess gasped. "Selena could never be involved in something like this. She just couldn't! For heaven's sake, Reed, you're talking about organized crime!"

Reed merely shrugged, but the burning in his gut belied his show of nonchalance. "Whether you believe me or not, your cousin was Edward Morrell's bookkeeper for almost four years. And that position has put her in deep trouble. You must know this wasn't her first trip to Grand Cayman."

She hesitated before she admitted, "Selena did mention that she'd been here before, but that's hardly an admission of guilt."

"Oh, she's been here, all right. Seven different trips in two years. Although no one will ever find any documentation to prove it, she was probably hauling Morrell's dirty money to the island's various banks and opening accounts in every one of them."

He hated the stricken look on her face. He remembered how Tess had always placed a high premium on loyalty, especially when she was championing the cause of an underdog. Unfortunately for her, this time she was attempting to defend someone unworthy of her loyalty, and something in her eyes—the sadness and disillusionment—told Reed she knew it.

"Do you know where she is?" he asked her again.

"No," she said softly. "I haven't seen her since she left our table." She glanced at her watch. "That was almost two hours ago."

Her face was too pretty to be so drawn with worry, and Reed couldn't help feeling responsible. "I hope I can count on you to help me convince her to do the right thing. She has to go back, Tess. The only way I can help her is if she agrees to cooperate."

She walked over to the window and with her back to him she said, "Why didn't she tell me? How could she be in this much trouble and not tell me?"

Reed felt his heart go out to the woman he'd once loved. There were a dozen good reasons why Selena Elliot hadn't confided in her cousin, and all of them were life threatening. "She couldn't tell you," he explained. "She would have been putting you at risk."

She spun around to face him. "But if what you're telling me is true, I'm already at risk, aren't I?"

Reed didn't try to dispute her logic, because he couldn't.

When she strode past him to the door, he caught up with her in two strides and covered her hand with his on the doorknob. They were standing so close he could almost taste her.

"Get out of my way," she said.

"Not until you tell me where you're going."

"I'm going to find my cousin," she informed him as she jerked her hand from beneath his. "Just as you should be trying to do if you were really interested in helping her."

He stood in front of the door, blocking her path, his feet braced and his arms folded over his chest. "No way, Tess. I can't have you poking around in something you know nothing about. There's too much at stake."

She scowled at him and flipped her hair over one shoulder with an indignant toss. It was a familiar gesture that sent him into a time warp of remembering.

"I'm not asking your permission, Reed."

God, but she was sexy. "Sit down, Tessa—"

"And will you please stop calling me that!"

"Sit down," he repeated firmly, his tone unyielding.

It came as no surprise that she ignored him and remained standing. "Will you please just listen," he said, working to sound more conciliatory. "Selena probably saw something or someone who spooked her. She's obviously hiding, and more than likely you'll be the one she'll contact when she feels it's safe."

He watched her silent and grudging acceptance of his logic.

"Think about it, Tess. If I found Selena, anyone else can."

He hadn't meant to scare her, but the alarm he saw spark in her pretty eyes told him he'd made his point.

"Stay here in case she tries to call you. I'll go take another look around the hotel grounds."

She sank down on the edge of the bed again, her shoulders slumped with the weight of the load he'd placed there. "If you find her, please call me. I have to talk to her."

He nodded. "Of course."

"And after you find her, then what?"

"It's my job to take her back to testify." He hoped she wouldn't ask him again if he was a cop. The thread of trust he'd just established was pathetically thin. If she pushed him to reveal the fact that he was a paid tracker—a bounty hunter—that fragile beginning would disintegrate like smoke in the wind.

"And what if she refuses to go back? What if she won't go with you?" she pressed him.

The eyes that met his were intelligent and assessing and he knew better than to try and lie. "Well, then I'll just have to convince her it's the best thing for her to do, won't I?"

"Stay here, Tess," he ordered at the door. "Don't make me have to go looking for you, as well."

"Go to hell, McKenna," she snapped. "And be forewarned that if Selena calls before you get back, I'm not making any promises or waiting around for your approval to talk to her about any of this."

He nodded, conceding her right to make both declarations.

Chapter Four

At sunset, the island sky became a canvas for an indescribable work of multicolored art, the likes of which Tess had never seen duplicated by man. But troubling thoughts robbed her of the joy nature's spectacle should have inspired this evening. As she stood on the balcony, gazing out over the water, Tess wondered how a dream vacation could have turned into a nightmare so quickly.

Below, dozens of people roamed the beach, couples walked hand in hand, kids frolicked in and out of the gentle surf and built fortresses in the wet sand. Among the other tourists enjoying the evening splendor was an older couple with a toddler in the shallow beach area cordoned off for small children. She would never have noticed them from this distance had Tess not been so be sure that the tall, dark, imposing figure standing over them was Reed. He seemed especially engrossed in conversation with the gray-haired couple, which seemed odd to Tess.

Was he questioning them about Selena? Had they seen her? Talked to her? Her glance swept the beach again and stopped when it found the tourist, whose stares she'd scorned this afternoon in the lobby, standing on the ground-floor patio outside the bar, staring up at her.

When he saw her looking down at him, he turned and walked purposefully back into the bar. Tess rubbed her arms, feeling suddenly vulnerable and inexplicably chilled, despite the seventy-plus temperature and the gentle southern breeze that warmed the evening air. When she looked back to the cordoned area where the older couple and the toddler were still sitting, Reed was gone.

As she continued to scan the area below for Selena, and now for Reed, the faint strains of reggae music rode the breeze around her. The jaunty rhythms that had welcomed and invigorated Tess hours earlier, now seemed teasing and cruel, a mocking reminder that while the rest of the island—at least that part of it vacationing here at West Palm—was spending a carefree evening, laughing, dancing and building memories beneath the Grand Cayman sunset, she was trapped in a frightening situation that she could neither control nor completely understand.

"Where are you, Selena?" she whispered. "And what in God's name have you done?"

Accepting that for now there would be no answers, Tess told herself to be patient, to maintain her faith in

Selena until all the facts were known. But despite her best resolve to maintain a positive attitude, the smattering of details Reed had given her swirled around in her mind and tested that faith severely.

The grim fact that the government had sent him to bring Selena back to testify was deeply disturbing, as was Reed's determination to find her. If the prosecution wanted Selena's testimony that badly, it seemed reasonable to Tess to assume that the defense would be just as desperate to keep her from giving it.

The dangerous scenarios that crept into her imagination made Tess curse every legal thriller she'd ever read. She cursed the quiet life she'd carved out for herself in Evergreen, the life that had kept her so preoccupied running her own business that she'd left little time for anything or anyone else. Despite the blood ties that bound them, Tess had to admit that she and Selena were little more than strangers. As Selena had so grimly pointed out earlier, it was true that they only saw each other at funerals. Since college, they'd done little more than exchange Christmas cards, Tess realized guiltily.

But even if she had made more of an effort to remain close, would Selena have confided in her? Tess wondered. And even if she had, how could Tess have helped?

When the phone rang, Tess jumped from the chair so quickly she knocked it over as she lunged back inside the room to grab the receiver before the second ring.

Her "hello" was clipped.

"T-Tess." Selena's strangled sob and a jumble of other incomprehensible words crackled through the receiver.

Tess's heart froze at the sound of her cousin's whimpers. "Selena! Where are you? What's happened?" Her own voice was shaky and her hand trembled as it gripped the phone.

A rustling sound coming across the line told Tess the phone had switched hands. "Your cousin is just fine, Ms. Elliot," a cool, calm, distinctly Caribbean male voice informed her. "Now listen carefully. In Selena's suitcase, hidden in the lining, is a book, a bound journal. Find it. Show it to no one. Do not attempt to copy or memorize any part of it. Tonight at ten o'clock bring it with you to this address."

Tess's knees bent involuntarily as she folded numbly to sit on the edge of the bed. *This isn't happening!* her mind whispered as she reached for a notepad and pen. *This isn't real. It can't be!*

"Are you still there?" The dispassionate caller seemed strangely polite.

"Yes—yes, go on," Tess managed to say.

"I will give you directions and instructions only once," the voice informed her, forcing Tess to concentrate on the situation that her hammering heart confirmed was all too terrifyingly real. "You will do exactly as I say, telling no one of our conversation, involving no one.''

"Just tell me what you want me to do," she pleaded. "I'll do anything, but please, please don't hurt her." She hadn't realized she was crying until she felt the tears drip onto the phone and seep between her fingers.

As the anonymous caller listed his demands and dictated a series of strange directions, Tess scribbled wildly. Although she hardly recognized the scrawl her trembling hand had produced as her own, she repeated the directions when Selena's abductor ordered her to do so.

"Ten o'clock sharp," he reminded her.

"Ten o'clock," Tess repeated as though hypnotized.

"Your cousin's life depends entirely upon you. We don't want to hurt anyone, but we will do what we have to do to get what we want. No doubt you'll be tempted to call the police, or maybe even go to your embassy. Do not consider doing either of those things, Ms. Elliot. If anyone accompanies you tonight, you will never see your cousin alive again."

Before Tess could respond to the horrifying warning, the line went dead. And for a long moment she could only sit with the receiver still in her hand, too numb and shaken and frightened to move.

Finally she hung up the phone, choking back the irrational fear that somehow by just disconnecting the line she'd severed her last tie to Selena.

Alone in the room that had grown murky with shadows, she felt utter despair. Her tears had ceased and in their place a cold, dry fear stung her eyes and burned her throat.

The numbers on the clock radio beside the bed glowed an eerie green. Seven forty-five. Selena's abductor had said Tess was to meet with him at ten. *Ten sharp.* The numbers changed: seven forty-six and with that change, the reality of precious time passing hit Tess with deadly meaning, jolting her into frantic action.

Once on her feet, she switched on the lamp beside the bed and dragged Selena's suitcases out of the closet and into the middle of the room.

Dropping to the floor beside the largest one, she jerked it open and sat staring, momentarily overwhelmed by the empty space staring back at her. She began searching. The stark fear that drove her caused her stomach to roil and her hands to shake as she felt the onset of a throbbing headache.

Although Tess was a frequent climber and had scaled some of the roughest terrain in Colorado, the obstacle she faced now was even more daunting than those lofty peaks. For Selena's sake, Tess prayed she was equal to the challenge.

MINUTES LATER, after patting the sides and the back of all three suitcases, Tess sat back on her heels, a feeling of defeat pressing down on her. She turned to the smaller carryon that Selena had brought with her, scolding herself for being so slow to think of it.

The journal had to be in the carryon, she told herself. Certainly if Selena *had* been carrying something valuable or incriminating, Tess reasoned, she wouldn't have checked it at the airport.

But after a thorough search failed to turn up anything concealed in the lining of Selena's smaller bag, Tess's heart sank again. In desperation, she searched all three suitcases again, ending with the largest one. She shook it, patted it and turned it upside down, but only after she'd kicked it angrily across the room and then stooped to retrieve it, did she feel the irregular outline on the bottom of the bag.

Her hands groped along the hard vinyl casing with trembling anticipation. Finally, she felt it: the outline of something firm and square and distinctly booklike lodged between the lining and the small, black plastic wheels on the bottom of the case.

Frantically she searched the room for something sharp to slit the lining, jerking open dresser drawers and rummaging through her own belongings. Finally, in the bathroom, her fingers closed around a metal nail file in the bottom of her cosmetic bag and a second later she was sawing away at the lining inside the suitcase.

When at last she withdrew the notebook from between the bag's cloth lining and the frame, her heart
beat double time as she stared down at the object that
verified so much of what Reed had told her.

Gingerly, she opened it and sat staring uncompre-
hending at row after row of handwritten figures and
dates, all recorded in Selena's distinctive left-hand
style. Reed had said she'd probably made numerous
deposits for Edward Morrell and, by the list of figures—many of them seven digits long—Tess realized
her cousin had been dealing with a substantial fortune.

Were the notations that stared back at her from Selena's journal the only documentation of Edward
Morrell's dirty money? Where had all that money
come from? And at what cost had this fortune been
amassed?

"Oh, Selena," she murmured, feeling heartsick and
hollow. "What have you done?"

When the figures began to swim before her eyes,
Tess swallowed and took a deep breath and told herself to prepare for the next step: the exchange of the
notebook for her cousin.

Panic rose inside her when it suddenly dawned that
she had no idea how she was going to find the rendezvous point Selena's abductor had described. She might
have given in to that panic, had she not glanced at the
clock radio and realized that time was slipping by. It
was already 8:15, which meant she had a little more

than an hour and a half to find the appointed meeting place, along streets she'd never traveled before, in a country where everyone drove on the opposite side of the road!

But as any good climber knew, when stuck in a tight spot, looking down was the first mistake. On the side of a mountain or in Grand Cayman, the only way out was up, Tess reminded herself with grim resolve.

Hastily she changed into a pair of jeans, a navy blue T-shirt and sneakers. With a last look around the room, she grabbed her purse, the scribbled directions for the ominous meeting place and Selena's journal, or the ransom, as she'd already come to think of it.

As she hurried toward the door, she shoved the journal into her purse and zipped the bag closed. The clock informed her that she now had little more than an hour to find the rendezvous point. Having no idea where the abductor's instructions would lead her, or how long it would take her to get there, made her mission all the more nerve-racking.

Right now all she could allow herself to think about was getting away from her room, away from West Palm and into the winding streets of Georgetown, where somewhere her cousin was being held against her will.

A knock on the door scattered her thoughts like buckshot. "Tess, open the door. It's me."

Reed! Tess's mind shrieked. Damn him! He would never let her get past him without an explanation of where she was going. And knowing him, if she ignored his pounding, he'd pick the lock or break down the door.

While she hesitated, wondering what to do, he banged on the door again, with more authority. "Tess. Open up. I know you're in there."

For one crazy moment Tess was seized with a bizarre impulse to fling open the door and throw herself into his arms and beg him to help her. But the bizarre and impossible impulse died when the ominous words of Selena's abductor came back to haunt her: *Your cousin's life depends entirely upon you.*

"Tess, let me in," Reed demanded.

"Just a minute," she stalled. "I'm—I'm not decent," she lied as she switched on the light and shoved Selena's suitcases under one of the queen-size beds.

"Tess. Open the door." It was the voice of a man unused to being kept waiting.

"All right. All right. I'm coming." She swallowed two huge gulps of air, willing her heart rate steady and pausing at the door just long enough to smooth her hair and whisper a silent prayer for courage.

"What's wrong?" he said before the door even closed behind him.

"You mean, *other* than the fact that my cousin is missing and you keep charging into my room?"

His shook his head and allowed himself a slow smile. "Never one to mince words, were you, Tessa?" The smile faded. "Has she contacted you?"

"Would I be here if she had?"

His curt nod was the only indication that he'd accepted her hedge. For the first time she noticed he carried a small canvas bag, which he tossed onto the bed before unzipping it.

When Tess realized that the bag was filled with his personal belongings she gasped, "What do you think you're doing?"

"I need a shave."

When he reached inside the duffel bag and withdrew a shaving kit, she blurted, "Well, go get one someplace else!"

He tucked the small shaving bag in one hand and turned to face her. "Listen, I've been up for thirty-six hours straight, I haven't had anything to eat or drink but airplane food and warm beer and I need a shower and a shave."

Tess was flabbergasted. "Surely you don't expect me to stand by and—and—"

"Watch?" He shot her a wicked smile and shrugged. "Suit yourself, Tessa."

"Oh! You are insufferable!"

"Hey, I'm not any happier about all of this than you are, babe. I'd hoped to fly in, snag Selena and be back in Miami by tomorrow morning. But sometimes we don't always get what we want, you know?"

"If you're so tired and so dirty, then why don't you go to your own room to bathe and take your stupid shower?'' she demanded. ''Give me your room number and I'll call you if I hear from her.''

His laugh was short, dry and brittle. ''You always were a lousy liar, Tessa. And as for the room, in case you hadn't noticed, it's the height of tourist season. There's not a spare room anywhere along Seven Mile Beach. Face it. You're stuck with me until your cousin turns up or you tell me where she is.''

''But...you can't stay here!''

''Too late. I've already moved in.''

She opened her mouth to protest, but he interrupted again.

''I promise I'll be out of here the moment I catch up to Selena. In the meantime, I'm part of the furniture.''

The man was not only insufferable, but infuriating, as well, and Tess would have loved nothing better than to tell him exactly what she thought of his boorish behavior. Right now, however, delivering the notebook still stuffed inside her purse took precedence over her anger and her desire to tell him off—now and over the past eight years.

The more pressing problem was how to get away from him to make the exchange with Selena's abductors. ''Whatever you say, Reed,'' she agreed suddenly, obviously astonishing him with her unexpected capitulation. ''There are plenty of towels in the cupboard above the john.''

The suspicion in his eyes was undisguised and she added a terse, "And please, put the lid down when you're finished in there."

He laughed. "I'll be the perfect guest," he assured her with a mocking bow. "I'm glad to see you acting so reasonably. You always were the practical one, weren't you, Tessa."

"I thought I asked you to stop calling me that," she shot back. "And I'll thank you to stop telling me what 'I always was.'" *As if you ever really knew,* she added bitterly to herself.

He nodded and continued to rummage for agonizing minutes through his duffel bag, withdrawing fresh clothes. Watching him, Tess couldn't help noting how his dark, expressive eyes glittered in the soft lamplight that cast his features in shadows—the high, wide forehead and the aquiline nose.

A slow, satisfied smile spread across his face when he caught her studying him. "You haven't changed either," he said quietly.

"Go on," she snapped. "Take your damn shower. I'll listen for the phone in case Selena calls."

He nodded and started for the bathroom with his shaving kit in hand and a fresh shirt thrown carelessly over his shoulder. Then he seemed suddenly to change his mind and headed instead for the door where, with a quick turn of his wrist, he locked the dead bolt with the key extending from it and withdrew the key and tucked it into the side pocket of his snug-fitting jeans.

Tess's heart stopped. She'd planned to slip out of the room the moment he stepped into the shower. When he turned and gave her a crooked grin, she fought to hide the panic she felt draining the blood from her face.

"Not that I don't trust you."

"I told you I'd let you know if Selena called." She forced her voice steady.

He arched one thick, sardonic brow. "And I'd like to believe you. It's just that I always like to cover my... bets."

She turned on her heel, marched out onto the balcony, plopped down on the chair and waited for the sound of water running.

"The offer's still open if you want to watch," he taunted before he closed the bathroom door.

"No thanks," she shouted. "I hate reruns."

She could imagine the wickedly triumphant grin that creased his handsome face, and the string of curses she muttered under her breath would have made a sailor blush.

Chapter Five

The minute she heard the water running in the shower, Tess reached up and unscrewed the light bulb illuminating the balcony, slid her purse strap over her arm, and peered over the railing, assessing her chances.

Her plan to escape the hotel by drawing on her free-climbing skills had been hastily conceived the moment Reed had chosen, in his patently caveman way, to make her a prisoner in her own room. It wasn't a plan without risk, but with a bit of luck it might work.

Most people were careful to lock their hotel rooms when they left them, but Tess was betting that most guests wouldn't concern themselves with the sliding doors that opened out onto a balcony several stories above ground level. It was a bet she was counting heavily upon as she prepared to drop down onto the small green roof of the balcony below her own.

If she couldn't gain access to the third floor through an open balcony door, she'd have to make the drop again, increasing the risk, not only of being seriously injured, but of being caught.

If the worst happened and she was forced to make the drop twice, she might well find herself trapped behind a locked sliding door on a first-floor balcony that was still a good twenty feet above the ground.

The graceful concrete archways and walkways that comprised the resort's mezzanine level would afford anything but a soft landing, but Tess steeled herself for the possibility that she might have to chance that final drop.

But of all of the dreadful scenarios that swarmed through her mind, the worst was the image of the inside of a Grand Cayman jail. If she was caught breaking into an empty hotel room via the balcony, how would she ever explain? Even worse, if she was caught, what would happen to Selena when she failed to make the rendezvous at the time dictated by the kidnapper?

Tess shrugged off the possibility of failure, telling herself that, dressed as she was in dark clothing, she'd be lost in the lengthening shadows of evening should an unsuspecting passerby happen to glance up. Not only was the darkness in her favor, but the fact that she was a good climber in excellent physical condition helped to buoy her spirits.

Although her plan of escape was frighteningly risky, she knew she had no other choice. Reed McKenna had seen to that, she reminded herself bitterly. Swallowing her fear, Tess took a deep breath and prayed that the first balcony she dropped onto would provide entry to an unoccupied room, which would ultimately give her access to the hallway and escape.

With one last adjustment of her shoulder bag, which contained Selena's ledger, Tess prepared to swing her long legs over the railing. But just as her foot came up even with the railing she heard voices coming from below. She stood frozen, her heart beating wildly.

Judging by the sounds of the happy chatter drifting up from the room below hers, a large group of revelers, giddy with West Palm's famous rum punch, had just emerged out onto the balcony through which Tess had hoped to make her escape.

With her mind scampering for another solution, Tess's eyes settled on a small strip of wood trim that ringed the side of the building and butted up against the railing of each balcony on the fourth floor. Before she lost her nerve or had time to consider the consequences of her hastily revised plan, she eased over the edge of the railing and gingerly transferred her weight to the small wooden strip.

The thin ledge upon which she balanced was flat and seemed stable, but it was narrow, no more than eight or ten inches wide.

Leaning into the nubby stucco wall, pressing her weight against the building, Tess prayed for balance and for the narrow ledge to be strong enough to support her one hundred and twenty-something pounds of weight.

Forcing herself to breathe while banishing one gruesome thought after another, Tess edged along the side of the building like the infamous cat burglars she admired so much in fiction. Cautiously sidestepping, moving first one foot and then the other, her hands searched the stucco for the slightest irregularity or chink into which her grasping fingers might dig and hold. Her purse scraped against the wall, further threatening her precarious balance.

The muscles in her arms and legs screamed with the impossible strain. Negotiating the treacherous course, Tess was haunted by the horrible memory of her last free-climb up the side of a stark, red sandstone monolith in western Colorado.

Her mouth went dry remembering the misstep that had spelled disaster that day—a thirty-foot free-fall that had resulted in a shattered ankle. The physical injury had taken months to heal, but the emotional scars of that expedition still lingered.

Despite her injuries, Tess had been the lucky one that day. Another member of the party had died when an unstable mancos ledge, some three hundred feet above a stark, boulder-strewn valley floor, had collapsed. Tess had witnessed the accident that had claimed the life of her friend Mark. Sitting a mere ten feet away, with her injured ankle splinted, waiting for the rest of the party to regroup and take her to the hospital, Tess had watched in utter horror as the thin crust upon which Mark had been standing, crumbled and collapsed.

The tragedy had happened three years ago. In the year before the accident, Tess had dated Mark. Their relationship was exclusive and becoming serious; they had even talked of marriage. Then, before her eyes, he'd been taken. Just as it seemed all the other people who'd ever mattered to Tess had been snatched from her life forever.

She hadn't been climbing since. In fact, she'd sold her gear and retired the Jeep she'd driven since high school. Since the accident, ideas of marriage or even serious dating had been far from her mind.

Without warning, her purse strap shifted and a jolt of adrenaline shot through her system, shaking her back to her present reality. *Snap out of it, Tess,* she warned herself as she stopped to regain mental and physical balance. This was no time to panic; no one knew better than an experienced free-climber how fear could paralyze. Paralysis was something she couldn't afford while hovering a hundred feet above ground, clinging to a skimpy ledge and a half inch of stucco.

Another few feet and she would be rewarded with success, Tess told herself. Steady. Steady. Just a few more feet. Cautiously, silently, forcing herself to breathe evenly, she edged closer to the balcony, which even from her precarious position on the ledge, appeared to be empty.

Another moment of torture and then it was over. Her hands had closed around the railing and her feet had landed on the balcony floor with no more than a gentle thud.

Trying to regain the edge that a rush of relief had dulled, Tess crept to the side of the sliding glass door. Her legs felt weak and her stomach churned as she peered tentatively into the dark, empty room beyond it. With trembling fingers, she tested the door.

It opened and she allowed herself a little inner yelp of triumph before moving on tiptoe across the dark hotel room.

At the door, she paused and listened before turning the knob and easing the door open a scant inch. The hinges were well oiled and she accomplished the movement noiselessly, but the sound of voices outside in the hallway caused her to shrink back into the shadows, where she watched through a slit in the door as the older man and woman she'd seen from her balcony walked past the room.

The woman walking beside him held the toddler in her arms and the man carried a plastic bucket and shovel. The child was fussing, on the verge of tears.

"Get her inside, Gertie," Tess heard the man say. "Before she draws attention to us."

Tess didn't have time to consider the remark she idly noted as strange before she seized the opportunity of the deserted hallway to emerge from the vacant room unseen.

A few minutes later she was in the resort's parking lot, trying to find the rental car Selena had turned over to the attendant when they'd arrived at West Palm. After a moment of frustrating disorientation, she spotted the red Mustang and hurried over to it, only to stop dead in her tracks when she realized she didn't have the keys. She'd never had them!

Naturally, since Selena had visited Grand Cayman before and was familiar with the route from the airport to the hotel, she'd been the one to drive. But remembering why she had no keys offered no consolation, and for one terrible moment, Tess felt that all was lost until she remembered the mopeds she'd seen people zipping around on as she and Selena had driven in from the airport.

"They rent them everywhere," Selena had explained. "We'll get a couple for at least a day. They're perfect for exploring the outer limits of the island."

Silently, Tess thanked her cousin for that vital piece of information as she raced the half mile to the main thoroughfare behind the hotel. Selena had been right about the availability of the popular scooters, and Tess had only jogged three blocks when she spotted a blinking sign advertising scooter rentals.

In less than fifteen minutes, Tess had filled out the necessary paperwork and paid for a twenty-four-hour rental of a noisy red moped. After a tentative trial ride around the lot, Tess emerged onto the highway and sped south toward the city limits, where her directions from Selena's abductors began.

As she road, the warm tropical night air swirled pleasantly around her, but her thoughts weren't on the atmosphere or the ocean air. Instead, her mind spun with the possibility of failure and her heart ached for relief.

But there would be no relief just yet. Not until she saw her cousin with her own eyes. Alive and well and out of danger.

IT HAD TAKEN every ounce of control Reed possessed not to shout when he'd stepped out onto the balcony and seen Tess inching along the side of the building like some kind of deranged circus performer.

No one had ever called Reed McKenna a religious man, but he'd nearly been driven to his knees at the sight of Tess balanced on the thin piece of wood trim a hundred feet above the ground.

He'd held his breath while she'd inched along, terrified to make a sound, lest he startle her and send her tumbling to, if not certain death, at least serious injury. When at last she swung one long, sexy leg and then the other over the edge of the railing that enclosed the neighboring balcony, he'd felt his whole body go limp with relief. An overwhelming desire to rush next door and either shake or kiss her senseless seized him.

But by the time he'd made it to the door, the cool professional inside him, the one that had taught him to survive in a business that would have broken a weaker man, had already reined in the impulse.

And now, with the stealth of a cat, he eased out into the hallway, slipped down to the second floor and waited beneath the open stairway for her to emerge. He almost choked when he saw Gertie and Jake and the baby climbing the stairs mere inches above his hiding place. If one of them spotted him, he'd lose his best chance of finding Selena Elliot. For he was ready to wager all that he owned that if he kept low and followed, Tess would lead him to exactly where he wanted to be.

Gertie and Jake walked past him unaware and went up to the third floor and into their own room. A moment later, Tess slipped down the stairs and hurried out into the hotel parking lot.

From a safe distance he watched her almost wilt when she realized the rental car would do her no good without the keys he'd seen her frantically searching her purse to find. Selena must have them, he told himself as he followed Tess to the moped rental. While she attended to the rental and practiced on the scooter, Reed ran back to the parking lot and hot-wired the Mustang.

Ten minutes later, he was following Tess toward Georgetown. She was driving too damn fast, he noted with growing concern and anger. If she didn't lay that rolling piece of tin on its side and break her pretty neck, he'd be pleasantly surprised. She'd always been too brave for her own good, he remembered, thinking back to that first night when he'd come upon her walking down the middle of a deserted mountain road, wearing high heels and a prom dress.

Despite himself, he winced, remembering how he'd been the one moving too fast that night, as was his habit. He'd been leaning into the curve, pushing the Harley well past a safe speed when suddenly in the glow of his headlight he saw an apparition in the middle of the road.

Had that fancy satin party dress of hers not reflected light like a mirror, he'd have run right over her and probably killed them both that night.

As it was, he'd barely kept from laying the bike on its side trying to avoid the beautiful prom queen standing like a startled deer in his path. After giving her hell for almost killing them, he'd listened as she'd explained between tears how her date with Jimmy Somebody had gone sour. Instead of driving her home after the prom, Jimmy had taken her up to the most well-known make-out spot on the mountain.

The bastard, as she'd kept calling him, had been drinking, they both had. But when he'd put his hand up her dress, Tess had shoved him and insisted that he take her home.

When he'd refused and grabbed her again and shoved her down onto the seat, she'd slugged him squarely in the face, breaking his nose, Reed had guessed, if the amount of blood on her ruined pink dress was any indication. He could still see that dress and her satisfied smile at the thought of the damage she'd inflicted on the overstimulated Jimmy.

After she'd decked him, Tess had haughtily climbed out of Jimmy's car and insisted on finding her own way home. Only when he'd left her had reality crashed down, reminding her that it was four good miles back to town.

It had been at that point in the story that Tess had started to cry again as she'd pulled up her dress to show Reed the pair of satin heels she'd ruined on the rough, gravel road. And it had been at that moment that Reed McKenna's heart had turned over, turning his mind to mush and making him believe that he could play hero to that endearing damsel in distress.

Even now, thinking back on that time of innocence, he felt moved by their young love. Within a few weeks, he'd become her first lover, and she had become his first and only real love.

With Tess he'd thought his life could be different. And for a while it had been; the things the old man did and said had hardly seemed to matter anymore.

The cocoon that Tess's love had spun around him held almost a year, before it began to unravel. Then all hell broke loose and the old man went too far and broke Sean's arm.

The courts had stepped in and with the help of Reed's testimony had taken Sean away. Just a short month later, Sean was gone forever. Stabbed by some strung-out punk in the backyard of the home where the courts had placed him for safekeeping.

The irony still stung and the lesson Sean's death had taught Reed was still indelibly printed on his mind: the old man had been right. Reed McKenna didn't really give a damn about anyone. He was incapable of caring enough to protect anyone. If he'd really cared for Sean, would he have let the courts take him away?

How could a man without a heart consider taking a wife, building a life with her when he hadn't even loved his brother enough to save him? Hadn't he promised Sean he'd always be there? But where had he been when his brother needed him most?

He'd given Sean up to strangers, even helped them take him away. In Reed's mind, it didn't matter that the old man had willingly signed the papers—Sean had never expected the old bastard to fight for him.

But Reed had always been Sean's champion, and if he lived to be a hundred, he'd never forget the look of bitter disappointment on Sean's young face when the woman from the county had come to take him away.

The flash of a signal light up ahead brought Reed back to his present situation with a jolt. He eased off the accelerator as Tess made a left turn and then another sharp right onto a narrow street lined with well-lit shops and open-air bars bursting with tourists.

Threading the rental car through the narrow street, Reed strained to keep the small red scooter in view. When a hotel limousine cut him off, Reed gave him the universal reply to rudeness and slammed on the brakes to avoid running down a gray-haired couple on a tandem bicycle. Although no one was the worse for the near-collision, Reed realized that in the confusion he'd lost sight of Tess.

At the next street, he turned right onto a wide paved boulevard lined with two- and three-story townhouses and condominiums. There was only one streetlight and very little traffic, so when Reed spotted a single taillight at the end of the next block, he figured he'd found Tess.

Following at a distance that wouldn't arouse her suspicions, he tailed the scooter through the three-block residential area. As they wove their way into the poorer section of town, the road became narrower and the pavement gave way to dirt.

Beyond a scattering of tin-roofed shanties, Reed saw the scooter's brake light come on and he eased off the accelerator and doused the Mustang's headlights. By the light of a pale crescent moon, he steered into a rutted driveway between an abandoned lean-to and what appeared to be a junkyard for boat and auto wreckage.

Once out of the car, he jogged back to the road where he'd seen the moped slowing. He spotted Tess's trim silhouette standing beside the scooter. She'd left the headlight on and where the weak yellow beam split the darkness it reflected off a small, corrugated-steel building. The warehouse sat alone in the middle of a large lot.

When Reed saw Tess walking toward the darkened building, he started walking toward her, moving quickly, keeping low, allowing his shadow to blend in with those of the bushes and palm trees that grew in wild profusion along both sides of the deserted road.

As he walked, Reed assessed the situation and every instinct he possessed confirmed that if ever there was a perfect place for a setup, this was it.

He crossed the street in order to swing around behind the warehouse unobserved. If Tess was walking into a trap, as he feared she might be, he intended to be in a position to intervene. As he jogged across the sand, he heard Tess calling in a ragged whisper, "Selena? Are you in there? Selena, it's me. It's Tess."

Just then the low groan of an engine refocused Reed's attention on a car as it turned onto the narrow road and headed toward the warehouse. Headlights sliced an eerie swath across the dunes behind him, nearly catching him in their glare had he not dived for the shadowy protection of the north side of the warehouse. Pressing his body flat against the building, he edged toward the entrance where Tess stood, alone and vulnerable.

Out of the corner of his eye, Reed saw the glint of steel as a gun barrel was shoved out of the window of the oncoming car. By the time he heard the first crack of gunfire, he was already running hell-bent and head down toward the woman standing in the line of fire. And by the time their eyes met, Reed feared he might be too late.

Chapter Six

"Tess! Look out!" At the sound of Reed's shouted warning, Tess spun around to see him charging toward her. Before she knew what had happened, he'd grabbed her around the waist and pulled her to the ground. It took a second before reality hit her. The crackling sound that peppered the air above their heads was gunfire! The bullets were aimed at her—and Reed McKenna had just saved her life!

"Come on," he shouted, dragging her with him as he scrambled to his feet.

Tess heard the car doors open and the sound of angry shouts and swearing. When she felt the bullets whizzing past them, her fear paralyzed all thought, but it triggered blessed adrenaline and pure instinct to which Tess reacted, running hand in hand with Reed, past the warehouse and across the soft, sandy stretch behind it.

She ran like a terrified animal, blindly, stumbling and gasping, too shocked and too frightened to know or care where they were going, and more than willing to let Reed dictate their course.

Her heart drummed so loudly, it was a moment before she realized the shooting had stopped.

"This way," Reed ordered. "Come on, Tess!" Still clutching her hand, he pulled her with him as he doubled back toward the road.

"They're leaving!" she gasped, running to keep up with him as she watched the speeding car's taillights disappear down the dusty dirt road. "Oh, Reed," she gasped, nearly frantic. "We've got to go after them! They've got Selena!"

By the time they reached the Mustang, Tess didn't have the time or the breath to ask how he'd come to be driving it. And once inside, she could only hang on when Reed floored the accelerator and the Mustang lunged forward, fishtailing across the soft dirt as the tires fought for traction.

By the glow of the dash lights, Tess stared at Reed. His mouth was set in a grim, hard line. He looked tough, angry and dangerous, and apprehension coiled in the pit of her stomach as her fingers dug into the armrest and she hung on for dear life. Trouble had always seemed to find Reed McKenna as a young man. Obviously, nothing had changed.

"Do you see them?" she asked.

"No, but I'm betting they're headed back to Georgetown. Did you get a look at the car?"

She shook her head. "With the headlights blinding me, I couldn't see much of anything."

"I didn't see much more, but from what I could make out, it looked like a limo, like the ones the hotels and dive tours send to the airport."

"Once they're back in town, we'll never spot them, will we?"

"It could be tough. Those hotel and resort limos are all over the island."

Tess strained her eyes to see as far in the distance as possible. The streets were virtually empty, but Reed continued to drive as though he'd drawn a bead on the limo with the gunmen inside. The speedometer read nearly ninety.

"It's obvious we've lost them." The despair rang in her voice. "You may as well back off the accelerator, McKenna. We won't be much good to Selena dead."

For the first time since they'd begun their futile chase, his expression changed and by the dim light, his smile appeared genuine. "You used to love to go fast, Tessa. What's the matter, lost your nerve?"

Unfortunately, her nerves were working all too well at the moment, as evidenced by the way he'd frazzled nearly every last one of them. "Slow down, damn it. You're driving like a lunatic. I don't appreciate you risking my life for your own cheap thrills."

He glanced at her, one dark brow arched sardonically. "And I don't appreciate being lied to." His smile had disappeared. That reckless and boyish grin that had once, and could so easily again, disarm her, was gone. In its place was a bitter sneer. The grown man Reed McKenna had become was a stranger. A hard, tough man, dangerous and capable of anything.

"And I don't appreciate being bullied," she shot back, despite the inner voice that warned her not to press him.

"Why didn't you tell me they'd contacted you?"

"You were in the shower, remember?"

"Damn it, woman! This isn't a game."

The tension stretched between them, vibrating and electric.

"They said they'd kill her," she said quietly. Merely saying the words had extinguished the fire inside her and robbed all the power from her voice.

His expression softened almost imperceptibly. "I need to know everything they said to you, Tessa," he said evenly. "Everything."

Their gazes locked for a significant moment before she looked away just in time to see an ancient pickup truck straddling the center stripe and heading right for them.

"Look out!" she screamed.

As he cranked the wheel hard to the right, Reed stomped the accelerator again. The Mustang responded and they flew around the limping pickup, sending two wheels into the deep sand on the narrow shoulder.

By the time Reed pulled out of the skid, they were already speeding toward a sharp curve. Instinctively, Tess knew they'd never make it. The engine screamed when Reed down shifted, but it was too late. They were moving too fast.

AS THE MUSTANG BUCKED off the pavement, Reed fought to control their skid. Crashing through the undergrowth, with the wheels grabbed and twisted by the sand, he somehow managed to keep the car upright until it came to a jarring stop beneath an ancient palm near the water's edge.

"Jesus," Reed muttered. "Are you all right, Tessa?"

Miraculously, she realized she was, but her mouth had gone too dry to speak. When the car had stopped, she'd been thrown forward in the seat, her head stopping inches from the windshield. "I—I think I'm fine," she finally managed to stammer. Physically, anyway. Inside her emotions were crumbling and she was shaking so hard her teeth chattered.

When Reed twisted around in the seat and brushed her hair away from her cheek, she felt her emotions reeling again. His fingers traced her jawline, coming to rest on her chin where the pad of his thumb stroked her lower lip. The concern she saw reflecting from his dark gaze subdued her trembling even as it set off another series of inner tremors of a very different kind.

"How about you?" she asked. "Are you okay?"

He brought his hand back to touch his own forehead where Tess could see a quarter-size lump forming.

She glanced at the rearview mirror that was twisted sideways. "You must have hit your head on the mirror," she said. "Are you bleeding? Let me see."

When she brushed back his hair to examine his forehead he caught her wrist and held it. As their eyes met, something familiar and warm and compelling passed between them. He released her abruptly as his gaze fell away from hers.

"I'm fine," he said sharply and opened the door. He climbed out of the car, closing the door behind him.

Tess joined him in front of the car where they both stared down at the twisted left wheel.

"I'm sure the frame's bent," he ventured. "I'll send a tow truck out in the morning." Tess's eyes followed his as he turned to gaze at the bank of lights that lined Seven Mile Beach in the distance. "We'll have to walk back to the hotel. Are you up to it?"

Tess nodded. "I'll get my purse."

"It isn't far," he told her. "Less than a mile if we follow the water."

They started out in silence. The moon was higher now, a sliver of silver in a velvet sky that cast a pale shimmering glow across the water. They'd walked five minutes in silence before Tess said, "It was a man who called . . . he said her life depended on me."

HALF AN HOUR LATER, sitting side by side on the beach looking out at the ocean, Tess finished filling Reed in on all the details of the call from Selena's abductors.

"Do you still have the notebook?" Reed asked.

She nodded. "I was supposed to bring it with me to the warehouse. He said I would be contacted there, given the rest of my instructions." She'd been contacted, all right, Tess thought angrily. But luckily the bullets had missed their mark. "Reed, what do you think will happen now?" She was surprised that her voice sounded as weak as she suddenly felt.

"More than likely, they'll contact you again. They achieved what they wanted to tonight, I think."

"Which was?"

"To make you a believer, to scare the hell out of you and make sure you followed their instructions to the letter."

It should have made her feel better, but instead Tess found Reed's ready answer strangely disturbing. To be so familiar with the kind of mind that could have orchestrated such a deliberate act of terror, said something about the way his own mind worked, as well, didn't it? At the same time, she had to admit at least a measure of relief knowing that Reed McKenna was not a man who would be easily surprised or taken in.

"They'll call again," he assured her. "My guess is they'll contact you tomorrow. We'll decide how to respond once we've heard their demands."

"We won't 'decide' anything!" Tess corrected. "I intend to do whatever they tell me to do, give them whatever they want. I couldn't live with myself if something happened to Selena." Her voice cracked.

"I need that notebook, Tess," he said flatly.

"I know."

The sound of the frothy surf combing the sand in front of them filled the dark silence with a series of soft, rhythmic sighs.

"For now, I'll settle for a copy. But eventually I'll need the original."

"To use as evidence against Selena," she said, feeling resentment gnawing at her insides.

"Maybe. Maybe not."

She couldn't look at him. "Meaning?"

"Meaning that if she agrees to come back and testify, the prosecutor will probably give her some kind of immunity against the incriminating evidence in that book."

"And so the notebook would only be used to substantiate her testimony against Morrell?"

When he didn't answer, the full implication of his silence hit her like a lead fist. "Or replace her testimony... if she doesn't... live to testify," she supplied for him, her voice betraying the horror that prospect brought with it. "Isn't that really why you want the notebook, Reed? In case Morrell's men kill Selena?"

Before she realized it she was on her feet and stalking away from him toward the hotel.

"Tess, wait."

He was beside her, but she wouldn't face him. "Forget it!" she snapped. "No notebook. No copies." When he grabbed her arm, she swung around with fire in her eyes. "Let me go!"

But instead of complying, he tightened his hold. "Listen to me, Tess. We have to work together."

"No! You listen! I don't have to do anything but try to save my cousin's life."

"Which you won't be able to do without my help," he informed her flatly.

"Oh really?" she snapped back, jerking free of his grasp. "Well, what if I said I think it was your interference that spooked Selena's abductors tonight and almost got me killed?"

"I'd say you know as well as I do that the whole rendezvous was a setup from the beginning. Believe me, you were a perfect target. If they'd wanted you dead, you would be."

She wouldn't give him the satisfaction of agreeing with him, nor could she say with absolute certainty that she did. Exasperated, she threw up her hands. "Look, all I know is that my cousin's life is in jeopardy and I've got to do everything I can to help her. I don't care two cents for that journal or what's in it. All I care about is finding Selena and getting off this island alive."

"And I can help you do just that, Tess."

"But how? I told you what the kidnapper said—that I was to tell no one and contact no authorities."

"And so far, they have no reason to believe you have. When those bullets started to fly, the limo was already leaving. I doubt they even saw me dragging you into the shadows. I said it before, Tess—if they'd wanted to do anything other than scare you, you wouldn't be here now."

God, how badly she wanted to believe he understood the situation as well as he appeared to.

"Whoever is holding Selena has a clear plan for how this thing is to be played out."

"You make it sound hopeless, as if we haven't a chance of rescuing my cousin."

"The situation isn't hopeless, but it is dangerous. Far too dangerous for you to try to handle on your own."

"And if I cooperate with you, my cousin could be murdered."

"And if you don't, she could be killed anyway. Are you willing to take that risk?"

Tess shuddered. "Of course not," she replied in a ragged whisper.

"Then you need to work with me, Tess."

"You make it sound easy."

He shook his head. "It won't be. But I want your cousin back safely almost as badly as you do."

"But for an entirely different reason," she reminded him.

"You're right," he admitted, unreasonably disappointing her when he did. "But what does it matter, so long as we both get what we want?"

Tess stared at him a long moment before she shook her head. "I guess it doesn't matter so long as we find Selena."

"Good. Now, here are the ground rules. You go nowhere, see no one, agree to nothing without consulting me—" when she started to protest he held up a hand to stop her "—and when the kidnappers call again, you'll tell me everything they say, no holding back, no more spider-woman tricks."

Despite their grim situation she had to smile.

Reed's expression remained deadly serious. "You can't play both sides of this thing and win, Tess. Either I call all the shots or we go our separate ways. And I think you saw tonight just how unprepared you are to deal with these people," he added for emphasis. "If we're lucky you get your cousin back, alive. And I get a crack at convincing her to go back to the States with me to testify." He held his hand out to her.

She thought a moment, remembering every bitter lesson he'd ever taught her about betrayal and abandonment. Shaking hands with Reed McKenna felt as though she were literally striking a deal with the devil.

What choice did she have? She was all alone in a foreign country, involved in a bizarre series of events over which she had no control. A criminal with a voice as cool as a banker's had threatened to kill Selena if Tess didn't do what he told her to do. But even when she'd complied, he'd terrorized her.

In his own way, Reed McKenna seemed to Tess to be as dangerous and unpredictable as the men who held Selena. But at least he was on the side wearing the white hats, she consoled herself. In the end, Tess realized she had no other choice. She took his hand.

"All right," she said. "It's a deal. But I keep the journal. I'll hand it over to you once Selena's safe—and not a moment sooner."

He didn't answer, and when she tried to withdraw her hand from his much larger, much warmer grip, he wouldn't let go, but held on even tighter and tugged her to him, close enough so that his dark gaze was inescapable. "I could force you to give it to me, you know."

Though shaken, Tess matched his stare without flinching. "I know. I don't think you would," she dared.

His eyes narrowed and she held her breath. "Don't be a fool, Tessa," he warned, his voice hard and low like cold steel wrapped in warm velvet. "You tried to make me into a hero once. It didn't work then, and it won't work now."

For a long dark moment his eyes held hers against her will.

"Then why should I trust you to help me?"

"Because you have something I want. I'm the same bastard you've hated for almost ten years, Tessa," he reminded her. "Self-serving and mercenary. You'd do well to remember that."

"I haven't forgotten for a second," she whispered over the lump swelling in her throat.

He released her hand abruptly. "Smart lady," he said, his unexpected smile surprisingly sad. "Just so we understand each other."

They walked in empty silence the rest of the way to the hotel and just before they climbed the wooden stairs that led up from the beach to the hotel grounds, he said, "We'll find her, Tessa," and slid his arm around her shoulders and hugged her against him.

The simple and completely unexpected act of compassion unnerved her and when she turned to look at him, she saw that he meant to kiss her.

At the first touch of his lips, the door behind which every memory of their time together was stored burst open. As though he'd sensed the change, he lifted his lips from hers for the space of a heartbeat, giving her the chance to pull back.

But even though his mouth had released her, his eyes still held her mesmerized, and when he settled his mouth over hers again and kissed her deeply, she responded with a hunger that rocked them both and left them breathless.

"Reed." She murmured his name and the spell was broken. He drew back so quickly she almost stumbled.

"We'd better go in," he said.

She could only nod and look away. Her voice was stolen by the series of sudden shocks rippling through her system. She felt dizzy, weakened by his kiss, by her body's own intense awareness of him. Numbly she followed him up to the room, her mind in turmoil and her heart in her throat.

In one short night, she'd cheated death on a narrow ledge, narrowly escaped an attack by armed assailants and survived a car crash that should have killed her.

In light of everything she'd endured, she ought to feel invincible, Tess told herself. Why then, she wondered as they walked into the hotel room and he closed the door behind them, had just one kiss from her former lover made her feel so utterly and hopelessly vulnerable?

Chapter Seven

For Reed, spending the night in the same room with Tess Elliot had been an exercise in self-control. He hadn't slept, hadn't even closed his eyes for longer than ten minutes, because every time he had, the image of her standing in front of that warehouse with bullets flying came back to him in chilling detail.

Though he longed to, Reed doubted he'd ever be able to forget how he'd felt at the thought of her dying. For a moment he thought his heart might explode.

The aftershock to his emotions had been even worse, resurrecting too many old feelings that were better off left for dead, or at least sleeping. Last night, instincts that were distinctly and disturbingly protective had been stirred and feelings he didn't want or need had begun smoldering again. A fire was beginning inside him that he hadn't allowed himself to feel for anyone since he'd left her.

He'd spent most of last night pacing and wishing to hell he had a cigarette. The more he'd paced the more he wanted her and the more he wanted her the harder he paced. The memory of how good she felt in his arms had taunted him through the long, dark hours and it still tortured him now.

With luck, Selena Elliot's abductors would contact Tess today and when they did, Reed meant to resolve the situation and get the hell out of Grand Cayman in the next twenty-four hours. He had to do something and do it fast. If Morrell's thugs didn't kill him, Reed warned himself, spending another night alone with Tess in separate beds certainly would.

As he moved past her bed and into the bathroom, he glanced down and saw that she'd slept fully clothed, with her purse, still containing Selena's notebook, tucked beneath her pillow. He could see the leather strap extending over the side of the bed and he couldn't resist smiling at her naiveté.

Did she really think if he wanted that journal badly enough a pillow would stop him? That sleeping in her clothes would stop either of them, if they wanted each other as badly as it seemed they had last night when they'd kissed? Reed forced himself to look away.

In the bathroom, he showered quickly and changed into a blue knit pullover and white shorts that unfortunately offered him no convenient place to conceal his shoulder holster or gun. For now, he'd have to be satisfied with keeping the .38 in his duffel bag.

By the time Reed stepped back into the room, the first pale rays of morning were filtering through the wooden blinds that covered the sliding glass door. Pushing the blinds aside, he stepped out onto the balcony and inhaled a lungful of ocean air. If things went well, fresh air would become part of his daily routine, he told himself, although the air he hoped to be breathing would be mountain air from the front porch of a cabin tucked somewhere high in the Rockies.

But even though his home state of Colorado beckoned him like an old friend, he had to admit that this island was pretty close to paradise, especially this morning bathed in the soft, pink light of a perfect sunrise. The only clouds were high and thin, and Reed guessed the temperature was already in the seventies.

The whisper of rustling sheets told him that Tess was beginning to stir. Before he went back inside, he took another deep breath and braced himself for the gut reaction he knew he'd feel when he saw her again.

She wasn't awake, but she'd turned over and kicked the sheets off her long, bare legs. She'd slept in an oversize man's white shirt and a pair of pink running shorts. An unwanted twinge of jealousy caused Reed to wonder whom the shirt belonged to.

Her long hair was tousled, but still silky where it fanned in thick swirls of dark brown against the white pillowcase. Her dark lashes lay like velvet shadows against her creamy skin.

The sight of her face, as captivating in repose as it was when animated with her indomitable spirit, touched Reed deeply and he remembered how much he once loved his beautiful Tessa. The term beautiful didn't really do justice in describing Tess Elliot, Reed decided as he sat down in the wicker chair opposite the bed. With her perfect bone structure, delicate features and skin as flawless and creamy as a child's, she was the kind of woman other women envied and men wove into their fantasies.

Unbidden, his thoughts drifted back to a perfect Sunday morning nine years ago when he'd picked her up on his Harley to take her hiking on a high-country trail behind her parent's home in Evergreen. It had been the first time they'd made love.

The memory caused desire to ripple in fresh waves through his body. As he watched, her dark eyelids fluttered open. "What is it? Is something wrong?" she asked, her voice husky with sleep and unbearably sexy.

"Nothing's wrong." His aching awareness of her made his response terse as he rose and walked to the door. "I was just going out to get us some breakfast." Until she'd opened her eyes, he'd planned on calling room service, but the sight of her, combined with his idiotic daydreaming, warned him to put some fast distance between them before he reacted again on impulse as he had last night.

"Lock the door behind me and don't let anyone in," he said over his shoulder. Before she had the chance to answer or he had the chance to look back, he walked out, slamming the door unnecessarily hard behind him.

THE OPEN-AIR RESTAURANT wasn't crowded, but Reed chose a small table in the corner to nurse a cup of black coffee while he waited for their breakfast order. Out of habit, his eyes flicked over his surroundings, assessing the situation for anything or anyone who could pose a threat.

He spotted and recognized Talbot immediately, even though the tall, sandy-haired agent had taken the precaution of dressing similarly to the members of the hotel staff.

Nick Talbot was Reed's age, thirty-one. He'd already been with the agency at least eight or nine years, recruited right out of college. They'd worked together during Reed's own brief stint on the federal payroll. Reed respected Nick, as much as he respected any of those by-the-book types who pledged blind allegiance to the bureaucrats. Even so, Talbot was something of an enigma.

In contrast to his mild temperament, Talbot's specialty was explosives. The few times that Reed had been assigned to a case with a bomber or a wacko with a penchant for chemicals, Nick had been the expert the agency called in.

Why, Reed wondered now, had Talbot been sent to Grand Cayman? What possible expertise could he bring to this case? Was it because of the way Andy Dianetti had been taken out in a blaze of glory? Perhaps the agency expected that same kind of attack on Selena. If so, why hadn't Charlie warned him?

Reed didn't have the information he needed to make any kind of definite assessment, but he did know that he had no intention of letting Nick Talbot into the middle of this case.

If a line opened up to negotiate with Selena's abductors, Reed would take the call. If Selena's incriminating journal had to be compromised, he'd sacrifice it. He'd watched the jury process work enough times to know that Selena Elliot's flesh-and-blood testimony would impress them far more than a book full of numbers, anyway.

The real question was, why had Morrell's forces taken this sudden detour? Why the focus on the journal?

Reed decided to let those questions simmer and to aim his immediate attention on confronting and removing Nick Talbot from the scene. He was out of his seat and halfway across the dining room when his waiter caught up to him with the breakfast Reed had ordered, all boxed and bagged and ready to take up to the room.

Reed hastily scratched a fictitious name and Tess's room number on the back of the tab, but by the time he glanced up, Nick Talbot was gone.

After a quick search of the lobby, Reed headed to a pay phone on the wall outside the men's room in the bar.

When Charlie answered, Reed said, "Call your boy in, Charlie."

"What? Who is this—hey, McKenna, is that you?" The fuzz in Charlie's voice told Reed he was the older agent's first call of the day.

"What the hell are you guys trying to do," Reed demanded, "get me and all your witnesses killed?"

"Wait a minute, hang on—" Charlie sputtered. "What are you talking about, Mac?"

"Talbot."

"Talbot? Nick Talbot? What about him? What's he got to do with this?"

"That's what I was about to ask him, right after he finished his rum punch."

"Nick Talbot's in Grand Cayman?"

"In the flesh, and looking about as convincing as a native as I'd look in a convent."

"I thought he was working the Dianetti case."

"You should have told me."

"Hey, believe me, Mac, if I'd known he had been called in to find the bookkeeper, I would have told you. I don't know why he's there. Honest."

Reed had learned from experience that most people only added "honest" when they were in the midst of telling a lie, but for some reason he couldn't name, he believed Charlie Franklin was telling the truth.

"Well, somebody had to have given him his orders, and whoever it was needs to get him the hell out of here," Reed demanded. "And by the way—" he dropped his voice a notch and cradled the phone closer "—Morrell's men grabbed the bookkeeper yesterday."

"Damn it!" Charlie shouted. "Do you have a link yet? Have they contacted the cousin?"

"Yes, in both cases."

"Is she willing to work with you?"

"She wasn't at first, but I think I may have changed her mind."

"Do you think the bookkeeper's still alive?"

"I think so."

"Strange. I mean, why? They certainly didn't give Dianetti a second chance."

"My thoughts exactly, Charlie." Reed didn't mention the incriminating journal. He sensed it was his trump card and until he was prepared to show his hand, the fewer people who knew of the existence of Selena Elliot's journal, the better.

"What are you going to do, Mac?"

"Whatever I have to."

"Anything I can do at this end to help you out?"

"I'll let you know. For now, just get Talbot out of my way before I have to."

Charlie groaned. "I'm going to pretend I didn't hear that."

"Pretend whatever you like, buddy. But I'm warning you, I've got too much at stake to let some G-man muck it up."

"What about the kid?"

"She's not your problem."

"The hell she isn't!" Charlie shouted. "I stuck my neck way out to get approval for you to take temporary custody. I just hope you had sense enough to stash her some place safe before you left the country."

Charlie's ulcer would explode like an overinflated balloon if he knew Reed had taken the child out of the country. "Are you trying to tell me how to do my job, old man? Maybe when I retire, you'd like to take over my clients?" Reed jabbed, diverting Charlie's questioning from a potentially dangerous route. "Ready to do a bit of free-lancing, Charlie?"

The older man's laugh was nothing but a cynical snort. "Mac, I wouldn't have your job for all the gold in Fort Knox."

BEFORE HEADING BACK to the room, Reed took another look around the lobby and the beach area for Nick Talbot. He knew it would be useless to ask for Talbot by name at the front desk. The agent, if he was registered at West Palm, would be using an alias.

Although he figured Talbot was long gone, Reed made another trip to the bar. Aside from a couple of waiters chatting with the bartender, the bar was empty.

Reed headed back to the room hoping that Charlie Franklin would act quickly and see to it that Talbot received his marching orders.

Reed had just turned the corner on the fourth-floor landing when a frantic Tess charging down the stairs nearly bowled him over.

When he regained his balance, he placed the take-out box on the floor and planted a hand on each of her shoulders to steady her. Tess's eyes were bright and her face was flushed.

"What's happened, Tess?"

"He called," she said, gulping to catch her breath. "You were right. He said last night was only a warning, a preview... of things to come if I didn't follow his instructions to the letter. He saw you, Reed. He said I'd double-crossed him." Her voice was tremulous and her breasts rose and fell beneath her blouse as she tried to catch her breath. "He said if he'd wanted to, he could have killed me. Killed you. And he reminded me that he could still kill Selena at any time—" Her voice cracked.

"Calm down, Tessa," he soothed as he turned her around gently and pulled her into the deserted hallway. "So far, he's only threatened. I know it's hard to believe, but you do still have bargaining power. You have what he wants—what they want, whoever they are. The kidnapper was telling the truth when he reminded you that if murder was his only intent, he had the perfect opportunity last night."

Once they were back inside the room with the door closed, he said, "All right, now, tell me exactly what happened."

Tess sat on the edge of the bed and took a deep breath. Reed could feel her physically trying to center herself, to recapture her poise, and his admiration for her grew. He'd worked with seasoned cops who couldn't recover from a shock as quickly.

"At first he was angry," she began. "But I told him I didn't know I'd been followed last night and he seemed to believe me. He seemed to *want* to believe me. Does that make sense?" Her eyes were wide and beseeching.

"Right now I don't think we have enough pieces of the puzzle to make a guess." He ran a hand idly through his hair. "Go on, Tessa. What else did he say?"

"Well, after warning me again to follow his instructions precisely, he gave me the name of a place where I'm to be given more instructions." She handed him a piece of hotel stationery on which she'd scrawled the name of a local bar.

"The Dive?"

She nodded and managed a weak smile. "He said there would be a message waiting for me there after ten tonight. He said to come alone and to identify myself to the bartender." She clasped her hands in her lap. "You can't go with me this time, Reed. They might be watching. I'll have to go alone."

Like hell you will, he thought, but resisted arguing with her for the moment. He would be there tonight, all right. And this time he had no intention of allowing her to walk into an ambush. From now on until this entire ordeal was over, he intended to stay one jump ahead of the game.

"Did he say anything else?"

"He reminded me that he held Selena's life in his hands," she said quietly. All color had drained from her face and beneath her eyes pale purple shadows attested to the strain under which she'd been operating for the last twenty-four hours.

Seeing her this way, shaken and afraid, Reed longed to get his hands on Selena's kidnappers and make them pay for the hell they were putting both women through. As far as he was concerned, the kind of men who bullied women were beneath contempt—men like his old man, gutless wonders who took their failures out on those they perceived to be weaker than themselves.

He felt his heart suddenly constrict as an image came to him of his mother—or at least the image of what he remembered her to be before his father had chased her out of their lives forever.

"Did you talk to Selena?" Reed asked, forcing himself back to the situation at hand.

She nodded and swallowed hard before she spoke. "Only for a minute. She was crying, but she said she was all right. She begged me to do whatever he asked.

She said he would do anything to get his hands on her journal and that I had to give it to him, no matter what." Her blue eyes swam with the tears he knew she was choking back. Without words she was asking him for reassurance, for comfort.

But all he could give her was the space to compose herself when she turned her back to him and walked onto the balcony. He watched as she stood in silence, staring out at the water.

Although his heart ached for her, he resisted the impulse to go to her. Kissing her last night had been a stupid mistake, one he couldn't afford to repeat. If she started believing in him, thinking they had some sort of connection or future, it would be just that much harder when she found out what he really was: a hardened man who would go to any extreme to get what he wanted, to satisfy his own purposes.

The best he could offer Tess Elliot was survival. He'd do everything to protect her and, when it was all over, get her off the island in one piece. But he'd proved long ago he couldn't live up to her expectations as some kind of hero. Even if he wanted her loyalty or her trust, he'd known for almost a lifetime that he deserved neither.

Reed McKenna was a man out for himself, he reminded himself. He got what he wanted at any cost. And right now, all he wanted was to find Selena Elliot, convince her to testify and collect his two hundred grand.

To allow his beautiful former lover to believe otherwise would be cruel. And even to consider believing it himself would be disastrous.

Chapter Eight

The hours until the rendezvous with Selena's kidnappers loomed before Tess like an uphill marathon, the waiting made all the more unbearable by the memories it evoked of that other horrible time of waiting with a loved one's life hanging in the balance.

Her mother and father had been killed outright in the crash, but her sister had lingered for three terrible days.

When Tess thought of Meredith, she couldn't help remembering the words she'd written in her diary before the fateful plane crash. The words came back to haunt Tess now, as though her sister had written them yesterday....

Dear Diary
I know I have neglected you, but things have been really wild around here. I just couldn't go another day without telling you. You see, I made a big decision today, a decision that will change my

life forever. I've decided to take Reed's advice and keep my baby. It will be hardest on Mom, but I just know she won't hate me. And Tess will be angry at first, but I know she will stick by me, too.

Reed says I'll make a wonderful mother. I'm so lucky to have him to talk to. I can tell him things I can't even tell you, dear diary. I wonder if I'll get horribly fat? Will I really wear those ugly tops when the time comes?

It sounds crazy, I know, but in a way I couldn't be happier. It is crazy, isn't it, dear diary, to believe that a sixteen-year-old can really become a woman just because she's having a baby. But last night Reed said I'm already the bravest woman he knows. I love him, diary. I guess I always have!

Later,
Meredith

Three days before the crash that claimed her family's lives, Reed McKenna had walked out on Tess. A month after her sister's death, Tess read Meredith's diary. And eight years later, Tess was still trying to forget what she'd read. But today, with Reed's magnetic presence so tangibly tempting, and last night as she'd lain in the darkness with the memory of his kiss still tingling on her lips, she'd forced herself to remember. *I'm so lucky to have him,* Meredith had written. Lucky, Tess thought bitterly, remembering when she'd felt the same way just being in love with Reed McKenna.

She stared at him now where he sat with his back to her on the balcony and she forced Meredith's words to play over and over in her mind like an incantation that would protect her from him and from her own weak will.

"I'm going for a walk," she said suddenly, grabbing her purse, which still contained Selena's journal.

Reed was beside her before she reached the door.

"Alone," she said over her shoulder.

"No way."

When she spun around to face him, an almost electric awareness of him sliced through her, further tuning her already humming senses. "Look, I need some air. I'm only going down to the beach."

"Fine. I love the beach." His mouth curved into a wry smile, shoving those damned appealing dimples into his cheeks again.

"You know, I think you're actually enjoying this."

"Yeah, well, you know how it is. Some guys just love their work."

She refused to look back at him as he followed her into the hall and closed the door behind them. A few moments later on the beach, Tess felt like an invisible observer, as far removed from the carefree tourists lounging and playing in the late afternoon sun as an alien stranded on a strange and unfamiliar planet. But at least out here among strangers, the tension of being locked in a hotel room with her former lover seemed to have subsided.

Tess walked purposefully away from a cluster of tourists relaxing on beach chairs. When Reed ducked under the thatched roof of a poolside bar, she slipped her purse strap over her shoulder, clutched her bag protectively against her and kept walking.

He caught up to her in a few minutes and she was fully aware of his presence beside her, but she resisted looking at him or acknowledging him except to shake her head at the bottle of beer he held out to her.

She saw him tip his own bottle up and take a long swig. When he stopped to take off his shoes she didn't slow down and when out of the corner of her eye she saw him strip off his shirt, she quickened her pace.

In a moment he'd caught up to her again and was matching her stride as they moved together along the shoreline.

"Must you keep following me?" she snapped.

"I told you I wasn't letting you out of my sight and I meant it."

She glanced at him and, despite herself, she allowed her gaze to linger a moment on his well-toned torso, on the stomach that was as flat and firm as it had been in high school. She scolded herself for remembering so much and for feeling so much.

"Surely I'm in no danger walking along a crowded beach in broad daylight," she insisted.

"Probably not in that getup."

She looked down at the loose-fitting T-shirt she wore knotted at the waist and the long cotton skirt that swirled around her ankles. "What's wrong with what I'm wearing?"

"Nothing. I just don't remember you being such a prude. You used to love the sun and, as I recall, no matter how little you wore, you never burned."

His unexpected reference to their past took her by surprise, but she recovered quickly. "You know, Reed, for a man who forgot his own wedding day, you seem to remember quite a bit of useless information about our past."

A spark of amusement danced in his dark eyes and his laugh was a low, cynical chuckle. "Touché, Tessa. But you know, now that you mention it, I think you're right. I do remember *some* things better than others. For example, I remember how great you used to look in a bikini. Let's see... the one I remember most vividly was a little black number, hardly more than a couple of strings that barely covered your—"

She stopped short and whirled around to glare at him, warning him away from completing his sentence.

His smile was knowing when he lifted his hand and let one finger skim the neckline of her T-shirt in a slow enticing manner that set off an unexpected shower of sparks inside her. "Have you stopped wearing bikinis, Tessa?"

Although his seductive teasing had turned Tess's insides to jelly, she wasn't about to let him know it. "No, McKenna, I haven't stopped wearing bikinis. As a matter of fact, I still favor the skimpy black ones." She tipped her chin and gave him an icy stare. "I have, however, stopped letting overheated adolescents help me out of them."

He arched one dark brow, his mouth curling into a deliciously wicked smile before he started to laugh. Unbidden, Tess felt a smile tugging at her own mouth. Despite her best resolve, she laughed with him.

"Sit down, Tessa," he said, smiling as he took her hand and pulled her down to sit beside him in the sand.

Tess sighed and hitched her skirt up to her knees, kicked off her shoes and buried her feet in the warm, wet sand. When he offered the beer again, she took it and drank deeply.

Without a word, they seemed to have agreed to a temporary truce and Tess welcomed the respite from the tension of the last day and a half.

As they sat side by side in the sand, sipping beer and staring out over the water, they fell into gentle reminiscing. Whether they liked it or not, they'd shared a past. A past that hadn't been all pain and regret.

She loved the sound of his laughter when she reminded him of the Halloween night he and Stan Olivetti had dragged an old outhouse into the middle of Main Street. "I thought the veins on Sheriff Cooper's neck would explode, he was so angry," she recalled, giggling.

She felt transported in time when he recalled how the whole town had gathered at the Elks' Lodge that Christmas when a blizzard had cut them off from the rest of the world for three days. "Sean was seven that year," Reed remembered. "He loved all the noise and confusion and having the other kids to play with."

Mrs. Slokum, they decided, was the most despised math teacher, and English teacher Ms. Perry had been everyone's favorite. Hank Vonn had brought the house down when he'd muffed his lines in the middle of the senior class play and Rudy Jones, Josh Kilmer and Patty Overfield had been responsible for putting the goat in the pantry in the home ec room. The tragic train wreck on homecoming night, 1983, had killed three of their friends and the senior class sneak that year had been canceled.

And so it went, the conversation flowing between them unforced, the feelings they stirred in each other nostalgic and warm, like going home.

When Tess finally glanced down at her watch, she realized they'd been talking for over an hour and that during that time they'd talked about everything and everyone but each other. A silence descended between them as they both focused on a riotous orange sunset in full progress.

The noise from the crowd at the open-air bar drifted between them and the smell of garlic and roast pork floated on the evening air, a subtle reminder of where they were and why they were together.

Tess sighed and allowed herself a final glimpse into her reverie. "I knew those people back home better than I knew my own cousin."

"But you lived with Selena's family for a while, didn't you?"

She nodded as she pulled her hair over her shoulder and idly braided it. "Yes. But Selena and I were never close. This trip was supposed to have been a new beginning."

He reached for her hand and squeezed it. "I'm sorry, Tessa." His tone was gentle, unguarded, almost sad, and Tess felt a sharp twinge of longing for the young man who used to confide his most secret dreams in just such a wistful tone.

"I'd hoped to confront Selena the day I arrived in Grand Cayman," he said. "If things had gone according to plan, you wouldn't have been involved in any of this. I might never have seen you again, Tessa."

She drew her knees up and wrapped her arms around them to suppress a deep inner shiver.

"Hey, let's get out of here," he blurted, standing suddenly and pulling her to her feet beside him. "It's almost eight and I want to scope out The Dive before your ten o'clock appointment."

Their brief sojourn into the past had temporarily distracted Tess from the seriousness of their situation, but now all her apprehensions and fears came back, redoubled in their intensity. "What if the kidnappers are watching? The caller insisted that I follow his instructions to the letter. If we go snooping around The Dive, we could be putting Selena's life in jeopardy. Besides, he may call the room again."

"They've made their contact for today," Reed said as they walked together back to the hotel. "And if they call, let them wonder. As long as we have that journal, we have a bargaining chip. They aren't about to throw that away."

Tess wasn't so easily convinced. "I think we should stay here," she argued when they reached the room.

"I have no intention of walking into another setup, Tess," he informed her. "I want to see that place before you go in. Now, go change into jeans or shorts. And grab a jacket."

When she made no move to comply with his order, he frowned, his dark eyes sparking and reminding her again that he was a man unaccustomed to having his judgment questioned.

Well, too bad, McKenna, she thought, *because I'm not a woman who follows orders blindly.*

As if he'd read her mind, he said, "If you fight me every time I make a suggestion, we're going to have a hell of a time trying to accomplish anything, Tess."

"A suggestion? You call that order you issued just now a suggestion?"

His eyes narrowed. "No. I guess I don't. All right, have it your way. I'm an insensitive pig. Now, go change. We can continue this power struggle after we've saved Selena's life.''

His blunt statement of what should have been her only concern hit its intended target dead center. She grabbed her clothes and stalked into the bathroom with her head held high.

He stood in the middle of the room, watching her go and muttering something about her stubbornness being the death of him, at which she allowed herself a secret smile.

A MOMENT LATER on the third floor landing they ran into the older couple Tess had seen Reed talking to on the beach yesterday. The woman carried the little girl, who twisted around and blurted, "Hi!" when she saw them. She was dressed in a pink ruffled sunsuit and in one small, dimpled fist she clutched a big red sucker with swirling white stripes.

"Well, hi there," Tess responded, smiling at the adorable little girl. "I see you've been to the beach and to the gift shop."

The child nodded enthusiastically, sending her honey-colored curls bouncing. "Big fishy out dere!" she announced. "My name's Crissy." Her blue eyes were as clear as the morning sky and as round as two saucers when she twisted around in the woman's arms to point a stubby finger toward the beach. "Beach!" she declared.

"She's adorable," Tess said. "You must be very proud."

The man's eyes flicked nervously to his wife's.

"Yes," the woman interjected, "her grandpa and I think she's pretty special."

"Down!" the child demanded, wriggling out of her grandmother's arms. The woman's expression was one of concern as she set the child down and reached for her hand, only to have the toddler shrug away from her and surprise them all by turning to Reed and holding her arms out to him.

"Up! Up!" she demanded. "Pick me up."

"Go ahead," Tess prompted when Reed hesitated. "Pick her up, Reed."

Tess couldn't help feeling a twinge of perverse pleasure at his obvious helplessness in the face of this persistent and disarming child. Finally, he relented, reaching down and lifting her into his arms with a gentleness that set off a barrage of poignant memories inside Tess. One of the qualities that had touched her so deeply all those years ago had been Reed McKenna's unexpected tenderness.

"She likes men," Crissy's grandmother explained as the child wrapped her arms around Reed's neck and pressed her peaches-and-cream cheek against his before offering him a lick of her lollipop.

Reed smiled—a real smile, this time—without a trace of cynicism or irony. When he pretended to gobble her sucker a cascade of laughter, like the sound of a wind chime, escaped Crissy's rosebud mouth.

Tess felt her heart swell, watching Reed with the toddler. In his eyes she caught a glimpse of the young Reed McKenna who'd once loved her. The real Reed, not the town's bad boy or the hard-edged man he'd become, but the Reed McKenna she'd trusted not only with her heart, but with her first real commitment of love.

"Perhaps she remembers you." Tess saw that simple suggestion trigger an inexplicable look of dark consternation to dart between the man and the woman.

"We'd better be going," the woman prompted curtly, reaching for the little girl. "Say goodbye to the nice folks, Crissy."

Instead of complying with her grandmother's wishes, the child shook her head and shouted, "No," before lunging at Tess, straining against Reed's arms. "Mama," she wailed. "Mama, mama, mama!"

Tess was almost as shocked by the child's outburst as her grandparents appeared to be.

"Come on, Crissy," her grandmother insisted, gently but firmly extracting the squirming, fussing child out of Reed's arms.

"Her mother's been...ill," Crissy's grandfather explained as his wife struggled to control the child who was still fighting to get to Tess.

When Crissy started to cry in earnest, her grandfather reached over and patted her back. "It's all right, baby," he soothed. "It's all right."

The three of them hurried in the opposite direction, leaving the echo of the child's pathetic cries in their wake.

"Mama!" they heard one last time, and the sound still tugged at Tess's heart as she followed Reed into the lobby.

"Poor little thing. She really misses her mother," she noted almost more to herself than to him. "She was a real charmer, though, wasn't she?"

Reed kept walking and didn't reply to her offhand observation. But the look on his face told Tess that his brief encounter with the toddler had affected him more deeply than she would have imagined.

Countless times over the years, Tess had wondered how Reed McKenna had reacted when he first learned of Meredith's death. Now she felt she finally had an answer.

Chapter Nine

"The Mustang's been towed," Reed informed her as he ushered her into the passenger side of the Jeep the valet brought round to them. "And I returned the moped to the rental agency this morning." He shot her a playful grimace. "Honestly, Tess, I thought I'd taught you better. After riding a Harley, I don't know how you tolerated that piece of plastic."

She shouldn't have let it, but his sudden friendliness and unexpected teasing made her feel infinitely better, easing the tension that was building in her shoulders again like a good back rub would've. "As you may remember, I didn't exactly have time to be choosy."

He smiled and nodded as he shoved the Jeep in gear and they jerked out of the driveway. Even with the breeze whipping through the ragtop Jeep and the sun setting behind them, the air was hot and humid and Tess was glad she'd chosen to wear a light pair of cotton shorts and a tank top. While Reed drove, she twisted her hair expertly into one long French braid down the back and secured it with a small barrette she found in the bottom of her purse.

Before closing her bag, she withdrew Selena's notebook, which she'd placed inside last night.

She felt Reed's eyes on her and on the journal. "You looked surprised to find it there," he said.

She'd never admit that she'd wondered more than once if he'd removed it. "Not really."

"Why not?" he asked, keeping one eye on the road. "You're not starting to trust me, are you, Tessa?"

She knew he was baiting her and she changed the subject. "No one calls me that anymore."

"Sorry. Force of habit."

She shrugged. "At first it bothered me," she admitted, "but now..." Her voice faded before she added hastily, "It really doesn't matter." It was a lie, but she was careful to keep her eyes focused elsewhere so that he couldn't read them, wouldn't see that another icy layer around her heart had melted.

HALF AN HOUR later the sky was almost completely dark, but when the Jeep's headlights hit it, Tess had no trouble reading the hand-lettered sign that read The Dive in garish, fluorescent green.

"There it is," she said. "Up ahead on the right." The long, low wooden structure seemed to tilt precariously to one side and yet miraculously managed to support a sagging tin roof. Along with a dozen other restaurants and bars, The Dive was situated on a beach above a midsize harbor where bobbing strings of lights revealed a cluster of commercial fishing rigs and dive boats docked.

In the distance Tess could see the twinkling lights of the modern high-rise office buildings in downtown Georgetown. She stared at the city's skyline and wondered how many times Selena had traveled this strip of highway to indulge in the shady business practices that had now put her life at risk. Tess had to swallow the resentment she felt rising.

Reed swung the Jeep into the sandy parking lot of a noticeably more upscale establishment a few hundred yards north of The Dive. They climbed out and walked around the building to the patio. A reggae band was in full Caribbean swing. The mellow music with its distinctive beat seemed again strangely irritating to Tess, whose jangled nerves begged for quiet.

They found an empty table and sat down. Reed ordered a beer and Tess followed suit, passing on the rum punch she knew she could never drink again without thinking of the day Selena had disappeared. When the waiter brought their drinks, Tess picked up a menu. An enticing spicy smell had greeted them as soon as they'd walked in, convincing Tess that she might be able to find an appetite with the right combination of foods.

"Take your time," Reed said after the waiter had left them alone again. "We have almost an hour before we're expected next door."

"We?"

He lifted his beer and took a thirsty swig before answering. "You saw that place. Do you really expect me to let you go in there alone?"

"But they'll recognize you from last night. He said—" Tess began in a whisper, feeling any hint of an appetite evaporate as her heart beat accelerated.

"I don't give a damn what he said," Reed interrupted in a burst of uncharacteristic emotion. "Besides, when I tackled you last night I was at a dead run. I doubt they got a long enough look at me to distinguish me from any other tourist wandering into the neighborhood bar to have a beer."

When she glared at him, he added, "Listen, I don't intend to advertise the fact that we're together, but you'll know I'm there should something go wrong." He drained his beer and stood up. "When the waiter comes back, order me another beer."

Tess opened her mouth to protest his leaving, but he stopped her. "Will you relax? I'm only going to the head. I'll be back before my drink gets warm."

THE DIVE was aptly named. Its atmosphere was dark and the lingering smell of stale cigarette smoke was almost enough to make Reed glad he'd quit. In one corner a group of locals played dominoes, while at another table a heated argument over a game of gin was turning ugly.

At the back of the bar, a group of loud drunks played pool beneath a plastic beer lamp that had yellowed with age and grime and cast off an eerie green light. From a jukebox beside the front door Willie Nelson crooned "You Were Always On My Mind." Idle curiosity caused Reed to wonder who among the assembled group had chosen the sentimental ballad.

When he walked up to the bar, he could feel a dozen eyes on his back and was glad he'd changed clothes before leaving the hotel and that the loose shirt he'd put on over his T-shirt now hid the gun shoved in his waistband.

Reed held up the bottle he'd brought in with him and indicated to the mahogany-skinned giant behind the bar to bring him another.

"Are you the owner of this place?" Reed asked the huge man whose full beard and shoulder-length hair was a dirty yellow-white.

"Yeah, mon," the bartender responded as he set Reed's beer down in front of him. "My name's Davey. Get it, mon? Davey's Dive?" The big man pitched his head back and broke into a hacking horselaugh. "Hey, you wouldn't be interested in buying Davey's Dive, would you, mon?" He eyed Reed hopefully. "She's always for sale, you know?" he explained, wiping his hands on the corner of the grimy apron stretched across his ample girth. "To the right man with the right money everything's for sale, you know what I mean, mon?''

When Reed didn't answer, Davey lowered his voice to a conspiratorial level. "But maybe you're looking to buy something else tonight, like maybe the company of a pretty lady?'' This time his laugh was low and dirty.

Reed shrugged and took a long, slow swig of his beer, while keeping one careful eye on the big man behind the bar. Experience had taught him that not all clowns were benign.

"I've been told that if I need to get a message to someone, this is the place to leave it. Is that true, Davey?''

The facade of friendliness slipped. "Message?'' Davey asked, leaning back against the row of bottles behind him and crossing his hamlike forearms over his stomach. "No, mon. We don't deliver no messages here." He shook his big hairy head and his eyes narrowed. "Maybe somebody's playing a joke on you or you got some bad advice. Or maybe you're just confused. You want a message delivered, you got to go down to the post office.''

Reluctantly, Reed pulled a fifty-dollar bill out of his shirt pocket and slid it across the bar.

With a look of undisguised greed, Davey eyed the bill.

"Take it,'' Reed instructed and when the bartender bent to pick up the money, Reed's hand snaked out and grabbed a handful of dirty beard and jerked the big man's face down level with his. "I'm here to pick up a message, *mon*," Reed mimicked in a menacing voice only he and the bartender could hear. "A message left for an American woman. Tess Elliot. And you're going to give me that message regardless of what you've been paid to do."

The man's eyes bulged and he opened his mouth, only to have Reed interrupt. "And after you give me that message, you're going to tell me everything about the scum who delivered it. Everything," he repeated in a voice dangerously low. "You'll remember him like he was your own father. You got that, *mon?* You got my message?"

The hulking bartender tried to nod, but Reed's grasp on his beard was unrelenting.

"Good. I knew I'd come to the right place." Reed sighed as he released the startled giant who stumbled backward rubbing his chin, his black eyes watering. "Now, talk. I haven't got all night."

When the bartender had finished talking, Reed knew little more than he had when he'd walked into The Dive. The young, black man Davey described as having left the cryptic message for Tess could have been any one of the dozen locals in that very room.

"You're sure all he said was to tell her to wait at the table near the jukebox and nothing more?"

"He said he'd be late—ten minutes or so. He said I should make sure she waited."

Reed put a twenty-dollar bill on top of the fifty.

"Let me get this straight," Reed began, "after this guy gives you the message he just walks out, right?"

Davey's eyes darted to the money and he shook his head. "No way. He finished his beer and played five or six songs on the jukebox. He really liked music, that mon. He hung over that thing, dropping in coins like he didn't ever want to leave. Then, like he forgot he had to be someplace else, he pays his bill and runs out."

"And he didn't talk to anyone, call anyone or meet anyone before he left?"

"No. But I wasn't watching him that close, you know, mon? I was busy. The fishing boats were docking and my regular customers were coming in."

Reed didn't take his eyes off the man, but he toyed with the bills on the bar in front of him, as if he might pick them up again. "I'd hoped you could be more helpful, Davey," Reed said.

Davey rubbed his heavy beard and tilted his head thoughtfully. "You know, there was one thing about him that I remember now that I think about it."

"Oh, yeah? What's that, Davey?" Reed asked, setting his beer down on top of the money.

"That mon, that messenger, he had the weirdest eyes. Gray—no, more silver, like a picture of an Eskimo's dog I saw once in a magazine. I ain't never seen no eyes like that on a black man before. But after this guy leaves, one of my customers—Elmo—he says he's seen the guy with the silver eyes down in Bodden Town. You know about that place, mon?''

"I've heard of it," Reed replied.

Davey sighed. "Lots of pretty women over in Bodden, you know, mon? They wear those little string bikinis and that's only when it's too cold to go naked." The hacking laugh started again, but Reed's scathing glance cut it off in midsnort.

"Has this dump got a back door?" Reed asked as he stuffed the two bills into Davey's shirt pocket.

The big man nodded. "Yeah, sure. Back that way," he said, pointing past a stack of boxes and garbage bags at the end of the bar.

"There's a number on the back of the fifty," Reed said. "If old silver-eyes comes back, you'll give me a call. Right, Davey?"

"Sure, mon." He patted his pocket and smiled. "But if I was you, I'd take a look around Bodden Town. Elmo, he knows everyone. If he says old silver-eyes comes from Bodden, then I believe him."

Reed downed the rest of his beer and headed for the door when a sudden movement to his left put all his senses on alert. Thanks to his old man, he'd developed a sixth sense for an ambush, and that gift came in handy now as he ducked the fist he saw coming at him while delivering a splitting right to the jaw and a punishing left to the midsection of his tattooed assailant.

He watched the tall, muscle-bound attacker reel backward, crash between two tables and flatten a wooden chair as he fell. The younger version of the bartender lay groaning on the dirty wooden floor.

Davey came lumbering around the end of the bar and doused the man on the floor with a pitcher of beer. The sound of chairs being scuffed back signaled to Reed that a couple of the gin players were headed his way.

"Hold on, boys!" Davey bellowed, his voice resounding like a foghorn around the room and stopping the men cold. "We got your message, mon," he assured Reed, coming up to stand beside him to stare down at the man who was struggling to sit up, huffing and panting like a wounded bull.

"I think you'd better be going now," Davey suggested. "This fool is my nephew—doesn't know when to quit, but I can't afford to lose no paying customers, you know, mon?" The horselaugh began again, this time backed up by a chorus of nervous laughter from the regulars who had gathered round to watch the show.

"You're all right, Davey," Reed said at the door. "I'll be waiting for your call."

When he stepped outside, Reed felt dirty and contaminated. Although his line of work often put him in similar settings, The Dive and places like it always made him feel like he needed a shower. He walked a few feet before he stopped to glance up at the night sky and take in a lungful of fresh air. It was a perfect island evening, warm and still, conditions that would be in his favor, since he didn't intend to let Tess out of his sight.

The thought of her dealing with the likes of Davey and his cohorts made his skin crawl, and no matter how much hell she raised, Reed wasn't about to let her walk in there blind, no more than he'd been willing to let her walk into that warehouse—or shooting gallery as it had turned out to be.

If he hadn't been thinking about her, he might not have jumped when he heard her scream. At first he thought it was only his imagination playing tricks on him, but his rage was all real when he burst back into the bar to see Tess shoved up against the jukebox with Davey's nephew towering over her, his big, thick fingers digging into the pale flesh of her upper arm.

"You tell that boyfriend of yours I'm waiting for him," the big man shouted in her face. "Anytime, anyplace!"

"How about now?" Reed hissed, as he slid up behind the man and pressed the barrel of his .38 against his neck.

The bar was stunned quiet and nothing moved but the overhead fan as it stirred the smoke-gray air. Davey's nephew, his lip still bloody from his encounter with Reed, stood stone still.

Reed shoved the gun barrel harder against his neck and the big man raised his hands slowly, as if under arrest, but suddenly he spun around with a speed and agility surprising for his size.

Before Reed could pull the trigger, Tess reacted, and when her knee made contact, the big man folded like an accordion made of cardboard, dropping to the floor clutching himself, cursing and bellowing in pain.

"Damn friendly place you've got here, Davey," Reed muttered over his shoulder as he backed Tess with him out the door. If he went the rest of his life without dealing with the kind of dirt inside Davey's Cayman Island Dive, Reed could die a happy man, he told himself as he emerged into the night air again, with his gun in one hand and Tess's trembling hand in the other.

By the time they reached the parking lot behind the restaurant where they'd left the Jeep, Tess had stopped shaking, but her blue eyes were still wide and staring and her face was devoid of color.

Despite all she'd just endured, he came down on her with both barrels. "How the hell could you have done such a damn-fool thing?" he demanded, pinning her with his stare as he stood with his back to the Jeep, his arms crossed over his chest. "Didn't I tell you to stay put?"

The color returned to her face in a rush of red. "You told me you were just going to the men's room," she shouted.

"It doesn't matter what I told you," he shot back. "You never listen anyway."

"Oh, so that's the real problem, isn't it? You're just ticked off because I disobeyed your order!"

"God, you always were the most—" He clenched his jaw to keep from saying it, from saying that she was the most maddeningly beautiful, independent and stubborn woman he'd ever known.

"Go ahead, Reed." Her glare was simmering, undaunted by the challenge of going toe-to-toe with him. "Say it! You hate that I have a mind of my own, that I insist on using my brain instead of blindly following your lead."

"I told you I'd be back."

"And I suppose you think that should have been good enough?"

He didn't answer.

"Well, excuse me, McKenna, but I had my doubts. You've run out on me before, remember?" She turned around and headed for the beach. "And by the way," she added without looking at him, "I thought we had a deal about Selena's journal." She spun around to face him, her eyes no longer simmering but shooting fire. "Or was that just another one of your lies?"

Before he could respond, she took off again, her long legs sprinting, seemingly without direction.

When he caught up to her, he grabbed her by the hand and spun her around to face him. "What about the journal? Where is it?"

"You know damn well where it is."

His gut did a slow twist as the implications of what she was saying hit him. "Tess," he said trying to remain calm. "If you're telling me you don't have Selena's journal, we're in big trouble."

Her mouth fell open. "But—but I thought—"

"You thought what?" The dread growing inside him became a palpable presence.

"When you didn't come back, I got up to leave the restaurant and found that my purse was gone."

"Are you sure you had it with you when we went in?"

"Positive. I remember sliding the strap over the back of my chair." Her eyes met his as the awful realization dawned. "Oh, my God! You mean you didn't take it? I just assumed you wanted a closer look...I thought you...Oh, God..." Her voice trailed off in horror.

Reed wanted to yell at her, to berate her for doubting him, to scald her for losing their only real link with Selena, for risking their only real leverage with the kidnappers. But the look on her face told him that nothing he could say could possibly make her feel any worse, any more guilty than she already did.

"Don't panic, Tess," he said, even as his own mind scrambled for perspective. "Maybe it isn't as bad as it seems."

"Not as bad?" she gasped. "You know as well as I do that Selena's notebook was the only thing keeping her alive. The only thing they wanted."

"Listen, no one but you and I know the notebook is missing."

She brought her hands up to her temples. "Then you don't think—"

"That it was Selena's kidnappers who stole it?" He shook his head. "I really doubt it. More than likely it was just some con working the restaurants and bars frequented by tourists. Have you looked at some of the shacks around here? An expensive leather bag like yours signals money to petty thieves."

She blew out a ragged breath. "Well, someone is going to be disappointed if money was what they were looking for. Other than some traveler's checks and my passport, that notebook was the only thing of real value."

"Obtaining another passport won't be a problem."

In her eyes he could see she was more than ready to be reassured.

"And other than Selena, the kidnappers and you and I, no one else could possibly know the significance of that journal. To anyone else the numbers inside are meaningless hieroglyphics."

Reed offered her a smile, despite his own misgivings. "Come on, let's take a walk. We've got fifteen minutes before we have to go back inside that rat hole, and we need to talk about how we're going to handle your meeting with the so-called messenger, how you're going to explain the missing journal if he asks for it."

They walked along the beach in silence before she stopped suddenly and turned to him. "Reed, with Selena's journal missing you have no choice but to take her back to testify, do you?" It wasn't really a question, but a statement of a fact they both knew full well.

"Yeah. It looks that way, doesn't it?"

Tess sighed. "I'm sorry now that I didn't let you at least copy the information inside. What will happen to the Morrell case without it?"

The Morrell case. He almost had to say it out loud to make it seem real again. Somehow in the last hour he'd forgotten all about Edward Morrell, the upcoming trial, even the money this case would bring him. His entire focus had been on protecting Tess, keeping her out of harm's way.

With her back in his life, Reed was beginning to see how easy it would be to start forgetting a great many things: like loneliness and self-loathing, and maybe even that part of his past that had kept him from her for all these years.

Seeing her standing there grieving something she perceived he'd lost touched him deeply and he pulled her into his arms. His heart swelled when she didn't pull away. "We'll get through this," he promised in a murmur against her hair. "Somehow we'll figure it all out. For now, let's forget about the notebook and just concentrate on what you're going to tell that messenger, how to stall him until we can find Selena."

But even as he assured her, he wondered if somehow he really could manage to forget everything but Tess, to allow himself to feel love again. And what about her? Her bitterness ran deep; he saw it in her eyes nearly every time she looked at him. Was there really a way to recapture the love and trust they'd once shared? Today on the beach, he'd almost allowed himself to start believing a fresh start might be possible. But was it? Or had the past now become Reed McKenna's greatest obstacle?

Without warning, she pulled out of his arms. "Reed, look. There's a limo in the parking lot and I think that man standing in the doorway of the bar drove it in."

His eyes followed hers to the front door of Davey's establishment.

The glow of a cigarette in the doorway partially illuminated someone's face. Reed shook his head. "I think that's Davey catching some fresh air."

He'd barely finished his sentence when the night was illuminated and the air reverberated with a deafening explosion.

Before their shocked eyes, the bar and the man standing in the doorway literally disappeared in a flash of angry flames.

Chapter Ten

The deafening belch of smoke and fire arced sky-
ward, tossing flaming debris in all directions. Reed
grabbed Tess's hand and led her quickly along the edge
of the dock, purposefully moving away from the
raining embers and the crowd of people who were
rushing out of the restaurant and bars to see what had
happened.

"This way," Reed shouted.

A siren wailed in the distance over the crackling of
burning timber and the sizzle and pop of liquor ex-
ploding in the flames. Reed paused in the bustling
chaos when he caught sight of a familiar face.

"What happened?" Reed asked one of the old men
he'd seen earlier playing dominoes inside The Dive.

The man shook his head and ran gnarled fingers
through his thinning gray hair before he said, "I just
left the bar. Davey had followed me to the door.
Halfway to my car—*kaboom!* And then this..." he

bent down over the man who lay deathly still at his feet. "Old Davey, he never hurt no one."

Davey's eyes rolled open and looked up at the people hovering around him. His black eyes rolled unseeing before finally they seemed to focus on Reed.

The acrid smell choked Tess and she covered her mouth with her hand. Her eyes stung and tears welled, making Reed a glistening presence before her as he knelt down beside the huge, bearded man. Tess bent down with him, her arm looped through his, holding on as though he were the only anchor in a hurricane.

"Hang on, Davey," Reed urged. "Help is on the way."

The bartender tried to smile, but his expression turned to a hideous grimace when the pain seized him.

"Who did this, Davey?" Reed asked. "What happened?"

At first the dying man seemed not to have understood Reed's question, but suddenly his eyes grew wide and he gasped, "It was...him, mon!" Davey winced, the pain obviously unbearable. "The one I told you about...the one...with the silver eyes." Davey closed his eyes and swallowed hard. "He...left old Davey...a helluva message on the old jukebox, eh mon?" he muttered with his eyes still closed.

The look on Reed's face was murderous when he stood and shoved through the crowd, his grip on Tess's hand almost painful. She didn't look back, but she knew instinctively that the ambulance, whose screaming sirens announced its arrival in the parking lot behind the bar, had arrived too late to save Davey.

A sudden rush of guilt washed over her. "That explosion was meant to kill *me*, wasn't it, Reed?" Her heart pounded so loudly in her ears her own voice sounded muffled and distant.

"I don't know," he said, but she knew he did.

He knew as well as she that the intended victim had escaped the horrible explosion at Davey's Dive and as they walked across the parking lot toward the Jeep, Tess wondered if Reed felt as battered and shaken as she did.

His face was set in a stern mask, his emotions held in check by his self-control and reserve, steely and impenetrable. He'd always reacted that way to pain—blocking it out, holding back. She remembered the times he'd shown up at her door, his lip split and his face bruised from a beating he'd endured at the hands of his father. His expressions of cold rage on those nights so long ago had etched the lines she saw slashed across his face tonight.

If he noticed her staring at him, he didn't show it, but merely opened her door and walked around to his side of the Jeep and got in behind the wheel.

A police car roared into the parking lot behind a fire truck, the screeching siren chilling, and the revolving red and white lights stark against the velvet night.

"Close your door," Reed ordered. "We're getting out of here."

Tess couldn't believe what she was hearing. "Shouldn't you at least talk to the police, Reed? Tell them what Davey told you?"

"There will be plenty of witnesses for the police to question. Now, close the door," he ordered again, his tone rough and angry.

She did as she was told, but continued to stare at him as he shoved the key in the ignition and gunned the engine to life. "I don't understand," she said as he guided the Jeep quickly out of the parking lot and onto the highway.

"I know you don't," he said. "But right now, I'd appreciate it if you could just ride this out and try to trust me, for once."

"Trust you," she murmured, shaking her head. If he only knew how badly she wished she could, how badly she needed to be able to lean on him, to count on him to help her through this nightmare. "I want to trust you, Reed. And I *am* trying. But with everything that's happened and now, with that man back there…dying… Why, Reed? Why didn't you stay and tell the police what you knew? You believe this is all related to Selena's kidnapping, right? Then why didn't you stay and try to work with the police? I can't imagine a fellow cop not wanting to help the authorities, even in a different country. I just don't get it, Reed." She felt helpless, unable to arrive at a logical explanation. "I want to understand. But to watch you running away like this—well, I just don't know what to believe anymore." When words failed her, she pleaded with her eyes for his understanding.

When he whipped the wheel to the right and pulled off the road, Tess was jolted against the dash. When he cut the engine and turned off the lights, she realized she was holding her breath.

By the intermittent light of passing traffic, she saw him studying his hands where they overlapped on the steering wheel. Finally he sighed and turned to her and reached over and touched a strand of hair that had fallen across her face. At his touch, Tess trembled.

"Better put your jacket on," he said with a husky tenderness so filled with caring it caused a burning lump to swell in Tess's throat. He stared at her, his eyes never leaving hers as she slipped into her jacket.

Against all common sense, but at the desperate bidding of her heart, she touched his face, letting her fingers trace the firm contour of his jaw before coming to rest against his lips. "Sometimes I think it's you who doesn't know how to trust, McKenna."

His hand came up to cover hers where it rested on his cheek. Taking both her hands in his, he said, "Listen, Tess, I know you have questions, and I can't answer them all. Not now, anyway. I can't explain everything that's happened or what may happen in the next few hours. There are things...circumstances... that don't involve you, things I can't explain right now. Hopefully we'll be able to nab the bastards that tried to kill you tonight. And then we can both get on with the rest of our lives. But for now, you'll just have to take my word that I'm doing everything in my power to bring Selena back safely."

She sensed that making such a declaration cost him dearly and although she still felt a long way from satisfied with his answers, Tess knew that for the moment it would have to be enough.

Without her mind's permission, her heart answered, "All right, Reed. I want to believe you. I'll try to be patient. But it won't be easy. I'm so afraid they'll hurt her."

He leaned across the darkness and pulled her into his arms, bringing the tears she was holding back close to spilling.

This is insanity, an inner voice warned, even as she leaned into his embrace. Didn't she have enough problems right now without tempting fate by falling in love again with Reed McKenna?

Trust him, he'd said. Believe him. But how could she believe a man who could drop out of her life without so much as a phone call? Who could betray her with her own sister and then leave town? Even as all the old tapes played over in her mind, Tess gave in to the temptation that drew her to him, that compelling chemistry that refused to be denied by old memories and old heartaches.

He lowered his face and she tipped hers up to meet his. He kissed her—a long, slow tantalizing kiss that kindled a startling blaze of desire inside her. With his lips he begged her to forget the past and ignore the future. Only the present mattered, her heart cried.

When a flash of headlights from an oncoming car illuminated the inside of the Jeep, Reed dragged his lips reluctantly from hers. "You could make a man forget himself, Tessa."

WHEN THEY PULLED UP in front of the hotel, the lobby was nearly deserted. "Go up to the room," he said. "And be sure you lock the door behind you."

Reaching into the front pocket of his jeans, he handed her the dead bolt key. "I've got something to check out and then I'll be right up and we'll decide where to go from here."

A niggling fear that he would run out on her again nagged at the back of her mind, but she ignored it. "I'm too tired to argue," she said wearily. "I don't know why, but I can't help but think things might look better after a shower." The smell of smoke clung to her skin, a constant reminder of her brush with death.

"Good idea," he said. "But don't get too comfortable," he warned, his voice low. "We're checking out tonight, so pack up and be ready to roll when I get back."

"Checking out?" Her voice was incredulous, and she grabbed his arm and pulled him to the corner of the lobby out of earshot of anyone who might be passing. "Do you think that's smart? When Morrell's men discover that I survived that explosion, they'll try to contact me again."

"And you want to be waiting for them to take another shot?"

She glared at him. Was this his idea of working together? "Of course not. But if they try to reach me, to offer a deal, an exchange of some kind for Selena..."

He shook his head. "It's gone way beyond that now, Tess. As you just reminded us both, they tried to kill you tonight," he said quietly. "And I don't have any intention of letting them have another chance. The ball's in our court now."

His comments did more to scare than reassure her, but she nodded and headed toward the stairs.

"Get packed," he said before leaving her. "I want to be on the road before midnight."

Numbly, Tess climbed the stairs. On the landing she stopped and looked back to see Reed talking to the clerk behind the front desk. Every instinct told her to watch him, to follow him, to be sure he wasn't running out on her. The old battle between common sense and her need to trust him raged inside her as she made her way to their room.

Reed dialed Gertie and Jake's room first, knowing he'd be waking them and regretting again the position he'd put them in by asking for their help and bringing them to Grand Cayman.

Jake answered and Reed knew he'd been sleeping. "Hello, sonny," Jake's greeting was characteristically upbeat, despite the hour.

"How's it going up there, Jake?"

"So far, so good. Gertie and I are having the time of our lives and that little girl couldn't be happier. No problems here, son."

Jake had started calling him "son" from that first night when Reed had showed up at their café on the interstate to apply for the dishwashing job advertised in the window. He'd been thirteen then, filled with a defiant spirit that his old man had not yet beaten out of him.

"I'm checking out, Jake," he murmured into the phone. "Things are heating up. I'll be in touch to let you know where I am and if you and Gertie need to move."

"All right, Reed. You go on and don't you worry about us. We're hanging in just fine."

Jake's easy manner was reassuring. Reed's father would have been about Jake's age, had he not managed to kill himself with the bottle before he'd hit fifty-five. But age was the only similarity between Jake Patterson and Reed McKenna, Sr., Reed reminded himself.

"I can't thank you and Gertie enough—" Reed began, a sudden rush of emotion crowding his heart.

"Aw, go on, now, son. You know we're glad to help out. And this little girl, why, she's no trouble at all.

Hang on a second—'' Reed heard Gertie saying something in the background, but he couldn't make out the words.

In a moment Jake was back on the line. ''Gertie says to tell you we're having the time of our lives. First vacation we ever had away from the café, you know. You making that last bank payment sure took the pressure off.''

''Yeah, well,'' Reed stammered. ''Anyway, I'm glad you're doing all right. You guys just take care, keep your eyes open. Remember if you smell anything suspicious, you take those tickets I gave you and put Gertie and the kid on the plane and don't look back until your feet are on Colorado soil.'' Before he'd left D.C., Reed had made financial arrangements that would take care of Crissy if the worst happened.

''I'll be in touch, Jake. Tomorrow or the next day. This thing is coming to a head real fast. In no time we'll all be breathing easy again.''

''Don't worry about a thing,'' Jake said as they both prepared to hang up. ''Oh—wait a minute. Gertie has something else to say.''

Reed smiled to himself; Gertie *always* had something else to say. The rustling on the line signaled the phone changing hands.

''Hello, son,'' Gertie breathed into the receiver. ''Say, the old man and me, we got us a bet. I say that pretty little gal we saw you with in the hallway is the one you almost married. He says she ain't. Now go ahead, tell me I'm right."

Reed shook his head, picturing Gertie's satisfied grin. "As always, Gertie, you're right as rain."

"See there," she said to the men on each end of the line. "Now, listen, son, you best grab hold of that little gal again. She's a good one, old Gertie can always tell. The only thing worse than a mistake is making it twice, you hear?"

"Yeah, I hear you, Gertie. Now, you two go back to bed. I'm sorry I woke you."

Reed hung up the phone mulling the simple wisdom of Gertie's remarks. How easy life would be if everything were only that straightforward. With a sigh, he picked up the phone again and punched in Charlie Franklin's number.

"You got something against letting me sleep, McKenna?" Charlie grumbled after he'd picked up the phone on the third ring.

Reed glanced at his watch to see that it was almost eleven-thirty. He was tired, stressed out and completely shaken that someone had tried to murder Tess. In short, he wasn't in the mood for apologies.

"Just tell me what you found out about Talbot, Charlie. Why's he here? Who sent him?"

"Whoa, hang on, Mac. First things first. Are you sure it was Talbot you saw?"

Charlie's question set an alarm screaming inside Reed's mind. "Of course I'm sure," he snapped. "What's the problem, Charlie?"

"The problem is, no one sent Talbot to Grand Cayman. So either you didn't see who you thought you saw or the guy's there on his own. If that's the case, nobody here can figure out why."

Reed closed his eyes and saw the explosion at Davey's. "Are you sure, Charlie? Who did you talk to?"

"Everyone but Talbot himself. Seems he's on leave. When I got nothing but blank stares from Talbot's own department, I went to the top."

Reed knew Charlie could be like a bloodhound when it came to tracking down a loose end. "So what do you think, Charlie? Is there something going on that I should know about?"

"As far as I can tell, nobody's jerking you around on this end, Mac. They don't have the inclination or the time. Morrell's lawyers have asked for the trial date to be moved up a week and it looks like the judge is going to grant them the motion. It's not looking good for the good guys," Charlie warned. "We need that bookkeeper's testimony or Morrell's going to walk, and if he does, heads will roll at the department."

Reed ignored that dire prediction and posed the question that had been burning in his mind since the explosion on the beach outside of Georgetown.

"Charlie, do you think it's possible that Talbot could have been bought by Morrell?"

He heard the veteran cop release a long tired breath before answering. "I suppose anything's possible, Mac, but it doesn't seem likely. Talbot came from money, didn't he? Fancy college, first in his class?"

"Yeah, Harvard, I think." But who could say what motivated a cop to go bad, Reed finished to himself.

"Yeah, well, if you find him, you tell him there are some folks in D.C. who have some serious questions to ask him, you know what I mean, Mac?"

But the phone had already gone dead and Reed McKenna was busy preparing his own list of questions for the elusive federal agent.

WHEN TESS OPENED the door she thought at first that she'd walked into the wrong hotel room. The wanton destruction that greeted her took her breath away.

Furniture had been overturned, the mattresses had been dragged from the beds and sliced open. The table lamps lay in jagged pieces on the floor and the pictures had been ripped from the walls.

As she backed out of the room slowly, her hands flew to her mouth and her eyes burned with the combination of the horrors she'd already experienced tonight and the violent destruction before her.

Her first instinct was to call hotel security, but she didn't make a move toward the lobby. Instead, she walked cautiously back into the room and closed the door behind her.

A glance at the open closet revealed that most of her clothes were gone. Gone, too, were Selena's clothes and her luggage. Reed's duffel bag and a few odd pieces of her own clothes remained, but Selena's things had all been stolen.

All that was left behind was the senseless, blatant destruction that caused hot anger to sizzle inside her. Even though her anger was numbing, Tess remained clearheaded enough to realize that hotel security or even the local police were no match for the individuals who had wreaked this havoc.

Besides, even if she trusted the island police to handle a case as dangerous and complex as Selena's kidnapping, how could she begin to answer all the questions they'd ask? Why hadn't she called them sooner? What about the journal and the theft of her purse and the explosion tonight in Georgetown? The thought of the Pandora's box she'd be opening made her dizzy.

Quickly packing her few remaining belongings into a small carryon that had been left behind, she reminded herself that the most important thing now was Selena's safety. In the lobby a few moments ago, Reed had hinted that he had a plan, a plan to act instead of merely reacting to the deadly situation into which they'd been unwillingly thrust. The ball was in their court, he'd said.

"All right, McKenna," she whispered. "Work your magic." He'd asked her to cooperate with him, to believe in him and, as she stood in the middle of the pillaged hotel room, it shocked her to realize that she'd handed control of the situation over to Reed from the beginning. Now that she'd made such a commitment, she was in much too deep to consider backing out.

"You're getting that second chance, Reed," she said with conviction.

And for Selena's sake, Tess could only pray he wouldn't let her down the way he had the last time she'd been fool enough to trust him.

Chapter Eleven

He saw her looking for him in the lobby and hurried over to meet her. Her face was pale and in her eyes he saw trouble. "What's happened, Tessa? You look as if you've seen a ghost."

"Are you ready to go?" she asked him, her demeanor strangely calm.

He took the duffel bag she passed him. In his other hand he held a bag of sandwiches and fruit he'd ordered to take back up to the room. "Yeah, I guess so. Where are the rest of your bags?"

"They're gone," she said, her voice level but low as she looped her arm through his and guided him out of the lobby onto the circular drive in front of the hotel. "Ask the valet to bring the Jeep around, McKenna. And don't ask me any questions, okay?"

He responded to her strange behavior by doing as she'd asked, following her lead and smiling at the attendant when he brought the Jeep around and ushered them into it.

When they were both inside with the doors closed, Tess turned to him and said, "Now, get us out of here, McKenna, before we get stuck with a hotel bill neither one of us can afford to pay."

A FEW MINUTES LATER on the highway outside Bodden Town, Tess finished telling Reed about the ransacked hotel room.

"It was a nightmare," she said, "like someone had gone through the room with a machete."

"I think that proves that it was a common thief who stole your purse out of the restaurant, don't you?"

Tess nodded. "Until this minute, I hadn't taken the time to put it together, but now I realize whoever trashed my hotel room was searching for Selena's journal."

"I only hope their search convinced them you still have it."

Tess nodded again, but said nothing.

"Grab the flashlight out of the glove compartment and check that map again, will you? I don't want to miss the turnoff."

According to the information he'd gleaned at the hotel, there were small beach houses scattered along an isolated strip of beach just a few miles outside Bodden Town. Although it had cost him a hundred dollars for the clerk and a promise of two hundred to a cousin in Bodden Town, Reed had arranged to rent one of the small, private cottages for the night.

A sidelong glance at Tess, at the uncharacteristic downturn of her pretty mouth, of the dark circles beneath her eyes and he was glad he'd been able to make the arrangements for a place to stay. She looked exhausted, and he was feeling the strain as well.

"Not much farther," Tess replied as she studied the crude map the hotel clerk had drawn. "Judging by those lights up ahead we should be pulling into the village in just a few minutes."

"Do you know the locals claim pirates stashed their treasure in Bodden Town?" Reed said, trying to lighten the heavy mood that had permeated the atmosphere inside the Jeep ever since Tess had told him about the break-in and vandalism of her hotel room.

Tess sighed. "Right now I'd trade all of Blackbeard's gold just to know that Selena was all right."

He reached for her hand and squeezed it. She rewarded him with a tired smile that sent a rush of warmth straight to his heart.

"According to this map, when we reach Bodden Town we're to bear to the right, toward the beach. The cutoff is supposed to be about four miles from the edge of town."

As they entered the small village, Tess felt apprehension closing like a vice around her heart. Her imagination had given her a frightening picture of the man with the silver eyes that Davey had described for Reed. That the man was in some way responsible for the explosion at Davey's bar, frightened Tess beyond any fear she'd ever experienced. Yet, here she was in Bodden Town for the precise purpose of finding this dangerous messenger.

"The clerk at West Palm told me his cousin's house was at the north end of town," Reed said, dragging Tess out of her morbid introspection. "See if you can make out any of these street signs."

In a few minutes, they found the residence where they were to pick up the key to the bungalow. When they pulled into the rutted drive, a dog the size of a small horse stood in the pool of light coming from a bare bulb beside the door and almost immediately lights came on inside the small, dilapidated house.

"Our innkeeper awaits," Reed said. "Stay here, I'll go get the key."

When the huge dog began edging toward the Jeep, growling and barking louder, Tess actually laughed. "That's the first order in two days that I don't mind obeying, McKenna."

His wry smile caused a spark of intimacy to flash between them, a spark that warmed Tess, even as it unsettled her. *Two* days, her mind whispered. How could she have allowed him to get so close to her heart so quickly when she'd spent eight long years resenting his memory and associating him with her deepest heartaches, when everything she knew of him told her he would hurt her again? When she knew full well that her next heartache would come when he walked out of her life again. And this time he would be walking out for good.

But why should she even care, her common sense begged to know. Surely the chemistry simmering between them was merely the result of their having been forced together under the most bizarre and stressful circumstances, of being thrown together in a situation where they could trust no one but each other. The intimacy came from fighting to achieve a common goal, the struggle to survive and ultimately to save Selena.

Surely these feelings were transitory, emotions erupting out of turmoil that had no effect on the future and couldn't change the past—a past Tess couldn't pretend never happened. Even if she'd wanted to, her memories of Meredith wouldn't let her forget.

If there was some way for Tess to forgive and forget how Reed had deserted her, she might be fool enough to try it. But how could she forgive him for deserting Meredith? It was a question without an answer, a question Tess was still asking herself ten minutes later when they were back on the road, headed for the bungalow Reed said the leasing agent had described as "quaint."

As they bumped along the ragged road in the darkness, Tess felt every jolt as if her spine were made of glass. Her muscles felt as though they'd been pummeled and the lack of sleep and food had conspired to give her a whopping headache.

"Better slow down," she warned as the road curved sharply to the left. "We don't want to miss the turn."

Reed eased off the accelerator and leaned forward over the wheel, studying the area intently. "I think that's it. Up ahead on the right. It looks like a marker of some kind."

The dilapidated wooden sign had been almost obliterated by the elements, but the words had been burned deeply into the wood and with the headlights shining on them, they were amazingly legible.

"Cave Cove," Tess muttered, "one mile. Jack's Bay, two miles."

"According to the leasing agent, the hills around Bodden Town are dotted with caves."

Right now, with mental and physical exhaustion pressing down on her, Tess would have settled for a cave if it had provided a safe place to rest. "How much farther?" she asked.

"We're supposed to follow the road—or what there is of it—until it dead-ends." Reed's voice echoed his own weariness and Tess felt suddenly overwhelmed by despair.

"God, this is just all so unreal!" she breathed, slumping back against the seat and bringing her hands up to cover her face. "Here we are, running around in the middle of the night, looking for a place to stay. And in the morning—if we somehow manage to survive the night—God only knows what we'll have to face." She pressed her palms into her tired eyes and released a sigh laden with frustration. "I don't know how much more of this I can take."

Reed put his arm across the back of the seat and kneaded the burning muscles knotted at the back of her neck. Though she fought against the feeling, the warmth of his touch soothed her.

"Listen, Tessa," he began, "things may not be as bleak as they seem. Whether you realize it or not, we do have a couple of advantages."

She twisted around to face him. "Really? I can't imagine what they could be, but please . . . if we have any edge at all, I'd love to hear what it is. Right now, I'd welcome any good news you'd care to share."

"Well, for one thing, Bodden Town isn't large. In fact, it's not a town at all, but a small village. A man as physically distinctive as the one we're looking for shouldn't be that hard to track down. I hope to cover a lot of ground tomorrow, ask a lot of questions. With luck we'll find him. But even if we don't, it shouldn't take long for word to get out that we're looking for him. Perhaps he'll come to us."

She groaned and fell back against the seat. "And that's supposed to make me feel *better?*"

"It should. Right now, the silver-eyed man who contacted Davey is our only link to Selena. It could be that he's not one of the abductors. Actually, I doubt he is. The kidnappers are smart, too smart to let themselves be identified the way this guy was identified by Davey. Chances are our messenger is a local, the kind who'll do anything for money, a courier who was unwittingly used by Morrell's men. If he can be bribed, our search could be over sooner than you think.''

Finding the messenger still seemed a mixed blessing to Tess. ''I can't help hoping we find him before he finds us.'' The dangerous scenarios that came to mind every time she tried to envision a confrontation between Reed and the silver-eyed man who had become a monster in her imagination made Tess's blood run cold.

Edward Morrell was an infamous crime boss; the ruthless tactics employed by his underlings were straight out of every detective novel Tess had ever read.

''Hang on,'' Reed said as he made a sharp turn and edged the Jeep onto a steep strip of rutted pavement where, after only a few hundred feet, the road had been brought to an abrupt end by a wooden barricade.

After pulling the vehicle into the protection of a cluster of gigantic royal palms, Reed turned off the ignition and reached around to grab his duffel bag, Tess's small bag and the sack of food he'd placed in the back seat.

''Bring the flashlight,'' he said. ''And pull on that door when you get out to be sure it's locked. I don't like the idea of leaving the Jeep here, but the leasing agent informed me that no four-wheel vehicles were allowed on the beach beyond the barricade.''

"Where's your Harley when you need it?" she quipped wearily.

THE STRIP of isolated beach seemed to stretch on forever in both directions. Except for the pale glimmer of silver moonlight skimming the water, nothing else moved. Tess knew that under different circumstances she might have found the peace and quiet welcome, but tonight the isolated beach seemed ominous. Even the surf seemed strangely muted, whispering as it fanned out across the sand before slipping back into the sea.

After the night of chaos, the tranquillity seemed eerie and, although she guessed the temperature was still hovering around seventy, Tess was glad Reed had suggested she bring her jacket.

They'd walked for less than a mile when the flashlight beam revealed the small, wooden bungalow with a sagging thatched roof. Even in the darkness, with only the thin beam of light from the flashlight, Tess could see that the word "quaint" had been used generously in describing the tiny cabin with the crooked screened-in porch.

But right now the little hut by the edge of the sea looked as welcoming as the home she'd grown up in.

Under different circumstances, Tess could see how this secluded spot would be the perfect honeymoon hideaway.

"Well, here we are," Reed said as he pulled open a squeaking screen door and walked across the porch before shoving the key into the lock of the wooden door behind it.

Tess followed him into the darkness. Her hand automatically searched and found a light switch on the wall beside the door. When the lights didn't come on, Reed explained. "According to our landlord, there's a generator out back that runs on gasoline. Tomorrow I'll see about getting it cranked up. There's supposed to be a small wooden boat out back, as well. I doubt we'll have time to explore any of the small coves along the shore, but it's there if we need it."

A match flared and in a moment the room was bathed in the soft light of an oil lamp. Reed switched off the flashlight and smiled. "Home sweet home."

Tess stood in the middle of the small room and took in her surroundings. The little bungalow seemed surprisingly clean, at least from what she could see by the dim light. A wicker couch and chair, laden with colorful pillows, were offset by a small coffee table and a footlocker that doubled as an end table.

The kitchen was comprised of a small refrigerator and an apartment-size stove lodged on each side of a deep sink. The dining room consisted of a wooden table and four metal chairs arranged opposite the stove.

Reed set the bag of sandwiches down on the narrow kitchen counter and lit a tall, narrow candle protruding from a wine bottle in the middle of the table. Two large windows were situated on each side of the front door and sheer, gauzy curtains covered each one.

Just off the small living room through an archway, Tess could see a bedroom—the only bedroom, she realized with an unexpected flutter in her chest.

While Reed set out the sandwiches and uncapped two bottles of beer, Tess lit another oil lamp and took it with her into the small, clean bathroom that was situated just off the bedroom. The shower was surprisingly large, but there was no tub. She turned on the single faucet and the groaning pipes eventually gave up a gush of cold, clear water.

Clean towels and washrags were folded and stacked on a wicker hamper by the door, along with a bar of scented soap. Tess worked the bar into a generous lather and washed her face and hands and then rinsed again and again with handfuls of cool water. When she finally emerged from the bathroom she felt immeasurably better.

Reed had opened the windows and the gentle sea breeze lifted the curtains and filled the bungalow with fresh, cool air.

"Dinner is served," he announced with a curt bow.

He'd spread their impromptu picnic of sandwiches and fruit on a colorful beach towel he'd draped over the coffee table. He'd found two more candles, lit them and placed them at each end of the table.

After he sat down on the small couch, he patted the cushion beside him. "Sit down, Tessa. You must be famished."

He handed her an open bottle of beer before he picked up his own and took a long swallow.

Tess sat down stiffly, feeling suddenly and uncomfortably aware of the way the candlelight played across his face, casting shadows that only served to enhance the classic line of his face and accentuate his good looks. Unwrapping her sandwich, she tried to concentrate on eating while out of the corner of her eye she was acutely aware of his every movement.

They ate in silence, their glances occasionally meeting.

Tess hardly ever drank beer, but one sip made her realize how incredibly thirsty she was and also how little she'd had to eat or drink since yesterday. The roast beef was thinly sliced and perfectly seasoned, layered generously between crusty French bread, and before she knew it, Tess had become absorbed in satisfying her hunger.

When they reached for an apple at the same time and their fingers collided. Reed smiled. "Go ahead, I'll eat the grapes."

She nodded, unreasonably self-conscious. The room seemed too small with the combination of Reed

McKenna's sensual presence and Tess's senses working overtime.

"You can shower first," he said, "although as you've probably already found out the water won't be warm. I should have that problem solved by tomorrow, however."

"You act as though we might be here another night." The thought occurred along with a lot of other implications that Tess didn't want to think about.

He shrugged. "I can't say for sure. If we have good luck and find our man right away, we could be out of here before you know it. If not . . ." The things he left unsaid landed squarely in the middle of Tess's mind.

"If we don't have some lead tomorrow, I think we should consider going to the police," Tess said, rising and gathering their sandwich wrappers and bottles to give herself something to do other than look at him.

"You really can't stand to be alone with me, can you, Tessa?"

His question surprised her. "Well—"

"You'd risk your cousin's life just to get away from me that much sooner?"

Her temper flared. "Go to hell, McKenna."

One perfect brow arched. "Been there."

"Oh, yes, I'd forgotten, Reed McKenna, tough guy, the one with the crummy childhood and the rotten father." She should have regretted her outburst when she saw his stare turn steely, but somehow she wasn't able to stop herself from wanting to hurt him. All the emotion of the last two days, all the tension and the fear and the uncertainty seemed to erupt at once. "Well, I've got a news flash for you, McKenna," she continued, "you weren't the only one hurting back then. We all had our privates hells, you know?"

He was standing in front of her almost before she realized. "I'm sorry about your family, Tessa," he said in a low voice still tinged with the anger she knew she'd sparked in him. "I'd just arrived at boot camp in Kentucky when I got the letter from a friend telling me what had happened. I didn't know for six weeks and by then..."

"What?" she snapped. "It was too late for condolences, for a phone call?"

He glared at her, the telltale muscle working overtime in his clenched jaw before he turned away from her, grabbed his duffel bag and headed for the bathroom. "I'll wash up first. You take the bed. I'll take the couch." His voice was strained with the control she could tell he was barely maintaining.

"Go ahead, Reed!" she snapped at his back. "Just walk away. After all, what else could I expect? Running away when things get hot is your style, isn't it? When things get too tough or too complicated."

He turned around and walked back into the room, covering the distance between them with lightning speed. His face was contorted with anger and his eyes were two black, burning coals.

"When you wouldn't answer my letters what was I supposed to do?"

"I opened the first one, the one you left taped to my door the day you left town, the one that said you had changed your mind about marrying me. I figured there wasn't much left to say after that." Tess hardly recognized the bitter voice as her own.

"As soon as I was allowed the privilege, I tried to call. I wanted to tell you how sorry I was about your family, but your phone had been disconnected and I found out you'd moved to Denver—"

Why he stopped so suddenly and why the look on his face changed from one of anger to complete frustration, she couldn't begin to understand.

"Oh, hell," he said, running his hands through his hair before turning his back to her again. "What does it matter now, anyway?"

"It matters," she said, her own voice so choked with emotion she could hardly speak. "It matters that you tried."

Slowly he turned back to her, the look on his face was a mirror of her own deep, inner pain.

"You never even told me about Sean." Her voice was no more than a ragged whisper, but he winced as though she'd shouted. "By the time I heard what had happened to him, you'd already left town. Your father said he didn't know where you'd gone." *And that he didn't give a damn if you ever came back,* Tess added to herself. "I'm sorry, Reed. I know you and Sean were very close."

An almost imperceptible nod told her he accepted her condolences the only way he could.

"I ran into an old high school friend last year and she told me your father died that winter in the veterans' hospital in D.C. I didn't know. When I lost Mom and Dad—" she swallowed hard "—and Meredith, I sort of lost track of everyone back home."

They only thing that moved between them was the shadow of the flickering candles. The silence was filled with the soft sighs of the surf, the rustle of the breeze as it slipped past the curtains and the unspoken recriminations of the past.

"Peggy Bishop." Reed finally muttered.

"What?"

"The high school friend, was it Peggy Bishop?" The slightest hint of a smile tugged at his full mouth.

"Why, yes...yes, it was Peggy. But how did you know?"

He shrugged and she could almost see the tension draining out of him as he stepped closer. "Because she always was the biggest gossip in town. Remember when she told her mother about the two of us skinny-dipping at Crystal Lake?" The smile bloomed at last and Tess answered it with one of her own.

"Oh, my gosh, I'd completely forgotten about that." She couldn't suppress a sigh as she was transported back to that clear, cold lake. "I don't think I've ever felt so cold in my life as I felt in that water."

His hands were on her shoulders and he seemed to be looking for something in her eyes. "As I remember it," he said, his voice raw and sexy, "we found a very effective way to thaw you out."

Her hands were on his waist when his mouth started its descent toward hers. Tess felt herself involuntarily stiffening.

"You don't trust me," he whispered, "and there's no reason you should. But you want me, Tessa. As badly as I want you."

Her eyes couldn't get enough of him, couldn't keep from devouring that chiseled bad-boy face, with its slashing dimples, dark brows and midnight eyes—intelligent, cunning, streetwise, eyes that reflected a troubled soul that had seen too much pain and too little joy. Eyes that were burning with desire and need and with just one look melted her resistance like sugar in the rain.

"I want you," he told her again as his arms slid around her and pulled her against his long, hard body. "Tessa." He murmured her name into her hair, his smoky voice sending ribbons of desire slipping through her.

When their mouths finally met, their kiss was the kiss of lovers too long denied. Their lips were warm, moist, open, seeking and finding, and seeking again. When his hands slid over her bottom and skimmed up under her blouse, his touch sent shivers of delight racing through her as his hands closed around her rib cage and his thumbs brushed the undersides of her breasts.

"Reed," she breathed against his lips and slid her arms around his neck and let her fingers tangle into his thick, dark hair. A groan, primal and foreign, came from deep within her throat and warned her that she was moments from losing control.

He seemed to sense the subtle change and he dragged his mouth from hers as if it pained him. Burying his face in her neck, he whispered, "I want you, Tess," before he took her hand and led her into the bedroom.

In the doorway, he kissed her once more. A quick, hot, breathless kiss that left them both panting. A promise. A warning. A last chance to turn and run. But Tess wasn't running. And she only hesitated a moment before moving into his arms again, telling herself that this moment might be all they ever had. If it was, her heart told her that this one moment would be worth a lifetime of regret in the morning.

Chapter Twelve

Tess awoke alone. Forcing her sleep-clouded mind clear, she sat up in the bed and saw the bag she'd packed last night sitting on a wooden chair in the corner. Reed's duffel bag was gone. And so was Reed.

Reaching for her oversize white shirt on the tiled floor where it had been hastily discarded last night, she felt a growing uneasiness gnawing at her.

The bedroom door was open and as she slid her arms into the shirt and swung her legs over the side of the bed, she called out, "McKenna, are you out there?" She despised the tentative, hopeful note she heard echoing around her.

Walking barefoot through the living room, she pulled the front door open and gazed out onto the screened porch. It was as empty as she was beginning to feel. Hurrying back inside, she took a pair of shorts and a T-shirt into the bathroom with her and quickly showered in cold water that told her Reed was not out back fixing the generator.

Ten minutes later she was dressed, with her hair still wet when she gathered it into a careless ponytail at her nape. The watch she'd left on the table beside the bed read a few minutes to ten.

Outside it was already hot, the sky pale blue and cloudless above a calm sea that sparkled as though it had been sprinkled with a million diamonds for as far as the eye could see. She called his name again, much louder this time, as her eyes swept the beach on both sides of the bungalow.

Behind the cabin a long sloping hill rose some two to three hundred feet. Tess shaded her eyes with the back of her hand and looked up, but could see no one moving on the hillside.

Feeling restless and unreasonably agitated, she decided to walk to where they'd left the Jeep parked last night. Remembering how anxious Reed had been to begin the search for the silver-eyed messenger, Tess told herself that he'd started that search without her. Perhaps he had gone into town to get started with the questions he seemed so sure would produce results.

The jog down the beach should have invigorated and restored her, but when she saw the Jeep parked under the palms, precisely where Reed had parked it last night, she felt weighted once again with worry. Judging by the tracks in the sand, the Jeep hadn't been moved.

Apprehension rose in earnest inside her. *Where was he?* Last night had proved to her that he was certainly in good enough physical condition to have walked back to Bodden Town, but why? Why walk when he had the Jeep? And if he'd taken his duffel bag, didn't that mean he wasn't planning to return?

The answer came back to her by degrees, despite her best efforts to ignore it. He'd left the Jeep because he didn't want to leave her stranded, because even a coward had *some* principles. And even though he couldn't face her this morning, he wouldn't leave her with no means of getting back to civilization.

Walking back to the bungalow, Tess felt alternately disappointed and enraged. Her pride had been battered, and suddenly her senses became fine-tuned as she realized what a deserted stretch of beach this really was. Every sound spooked her, the sudden squeak of a bird, the tide hissing around a rock, even the breeze rustling through the stately palms.

By the time she stepped back across the screened porch and into the house, her nerves were stretched as taut as violin strings. If Reed McKenna didn't show up in the next hour, she vowed to drive back to Georgetown and lay the whole matter at the feet of the Cayman police, whether he approved or not.

She killed five minutes by making the bed, and another five by clearing the remnants of last night's picnic dinner from the living room. Then, left alone with the time moving in slow motion, her mind began to whirl again with possible explanations for Reed's absence.

She walked out onto the porch and stared at the sea as her thoughts drifted back to their lovemaking last night. Closing her eyes, she could almost imagine the warmth of his breath on her cheek, the touch of his hands on her skin.

Their lovemaking had gone from the heated urgency of lost teenage lovers, to the slow, patient reacquainting of the adults they had become. Their kisses had been soft, deep, thorough... then touching, tender. Though Reed's body had been taut and hard, his caresses had been as sensual as fine silk.

He had held her and kissed her like a man deeply in love, and by the light of the flickering candles, she'd seen in his eyes the depth of his need. Physical. Spiritual. His soul was now as battered as his young body had once been.

When the first pink light of morning had begun to seep around the curtains at the bedroom window, they'd held each other and fallen into a deep satisfied sleep, entwined in each others' arms, their sated bodies still moist with spent passion.

But all the remembered tenderness and ecstasy of last night could not dispel the hard reality of the morning that Tess stood facing alone. And although she fought to resist it, a single thought repeated itself over and over in her mind: *he left you again*. He could not face her, could not face the adult demands he imagined she might make on him after last night's intimacies.

Tess berated first herself and then him as she tossed her clothes into her bag and proceeded to search for the keys to the Jeep.

Eventually she found them under the bed, where she figured they must have fallen from Reed's pocket when she'd undressed him last night. Her humiliation and rage rose like a geyser at the thought that he'd been in such a rush to leave her this morning that he hadn't taken the time to look for the keys.

By the time she heard the motorcycle pull up in front of the bungalow, she was already across the porch, propelled by a head of angry steam that would not be quelled. Her whole body was shaking with the unspoken accusations that she longed to hurl at him. And when she saw him riding toward her, shirtless, his tanned chest glistening in the morning sun, his dark hair shining and tousled by the breeze, his easy smile carving dimples in his cheeks, she felt her heart breaking.

THE FIRST THING he saw when he shut off the engine was her bag and the keys to the Jeep clutched in her hand. The next thing he noticed, besides her slightly swollen lower lip and the tantalizing way she looked standing in snug-fitting blue-jean shorts and bare feet, was the look on her face. The expression she wore was one of blatant anger, a look of sheer rage that he couldn't begin to understand.

"Where are you going, Tessa?"

"What the hell do you care?" Her eyes had turned a deeper blue and her face was flushed with crimson.

"Hey, what's going on? What's happened?" he asked, placing a hand on each shoulder, only to feel her go rigid beneath his touch.

"That might be a more appropriate question for me to be asking, don't you think, Reed? I've been shot at and chased. I've been the target of an explosion that killed at least one innocent man. I'm standing here in the middle of nowhere with my only living relative missing, at the mercy of cold-blooded gangsters, and you have the gall to ask me what's going on?" She stopped only long enough to drag in a lungful of air. "And as if all of that isn't bad enough, I wake up this morning to find you gone, God knows where, without a word. The man who just last night asked me to trust him, despite the fact that he not only left me at the altar, but betrayed me in the most heartless way—" The tears welled, but she refused to let them fall.

"Betrayed you? Tessa, I—"

She swiped savagely at her eyes and shoved past him. "Get out of my way, McKenna. I'm going back to Georgetown and straight to the police, which is where I should have gone when I first discovered Selena was missing."

He grabbed her arm, but she shrugged away from him. "Get out of my way, McKenna," she repeated.

"And don't try to stop me from doing what I know now I have to do."

"I won't try to stop you from doing anything, but I think I deserve some kind of an explanation for why you shared my bed last night, and this morning I've suddenly become your enemy again."

Her eyes were dry, the tears gone, replaced by an expression of bitterness that caused his heart to constrict painfully in his chest. "*You* want an explanation?" she gasped, her indignation a formidable presence between them. "You know, Reed, coming from you that's almost funny, from the man famous for his walking act, for disappearing just when he's most needed."

He felt his own anger rising at the need to explain himself, but he fought to control his temper. "This morning when the leasing agent came by, I didn't want to wake you. I rode back into town with him to pick up gasoline for the generator. I rented this bike, figuring we could cover more ground if we split up today to question the locals."

Her eyes flicked to the metal gas can strapped to the back of the bike. "I didn't leave you, Tessa."

"No," she admitted, "you didn't leave me...not this time. But the point is, you could have. And the problem is, I'd care if you did!" She turned to stare out over the water, crossing her arms protectively over her heart. "I can't let myself believe in you, McKenna. This morning, waking up alone..." Her voice caught and she swallowed hard before continuing. "Well, it just all came back, that's all," she said quietly. "I know I have no right to expect anything from you, to hope for anything. You haven't made any promises and neither have I."

He came up behind her and put his hands on her shoulders. "I'm sorry, Tessa." He could almost feel the past coming between them again.

They'd started planning the wedding that January. The date had been set for mid-June. The invitations had been ordered and she'd even picked out a dress. But then Sean had been killed.

"When Sean died I felt responsible." Just saying the words twisted a knot in his heart. "I let him down. He thought I'd always be there for him. I couldn't take the chance that I'd do the same thing to you." He'd admitted more to her in thirty seconds than he'd ever admitted to anyone, including himself, in eight years.

"Running away, enlisting...it was a cowardly thing to do, I know that now. And I admit it. I'm sorry. You deserved better. Much better than I could ever give you." He let his hands fall away from her shoulders, but she didn't walk away. At least she was willing to hear him out and that alone was something, he told himself as he continued trying to reach her.

"I was young, stupid, a coward—all the things you thought about me and more were true. But damn it, Tess, young people break engagements every day. To hate me for so long, to carry around all this bitterness . . . Tess, how could you hate me for so long?''

When her eyes met his again, they were accusing.

''I don't know how you can stand there and pretend not to know.''

He had no answer for something he didn't understand.

''She was so young, and she loved you so much.'' She swallowed the emotion he could hear choking her. ''Okay, so you decided you couldn't marry me—all right. I understand. And I learned to live with it. But my God, Reed, how could you just walk out on her like that? Just pretend she never existed, that the child she was carrying never happened?''

If she'd slapped him he couldn't have felt more stunned. ''Child?'' he blurted. ''What child?'' His mind scrambled in a dozen different directions at the same time, but for the life of him he had no idea who or what she was talking about.

With a final look of bitterness and disgust, she turned and started walking toward the road.

''Wait. Tess! Wait, damn it!''

''Forget it, McKenna,'' she shouted over her shoulder.

Standing there, watching her go, his mind raced back in time, working frantically to make some sense out of the things she'd said. *The child she was carrying . . .* Was it possible that someone had lied to Tess, told her he'd been unfaithful? But who? *The child she was carrying…she was so young…* The puzzle pieces fell together, but the picture they formed was distorted.

When he caught up to her, he didn't try to stop her or touch her, but merely matched her stride, watching her chest rise and fall with every angry breath and feeling his own frustration straining to the breaking point.

"Are you telling me you thought Meredith was carrying my child?"

She kept walking and didn't answer.

"But you can't seriously believe that!"

"I can't?" she blurted, stopping so suddenly he almost stumbled into her.

"No, you can't believe it. Because it isn't true. Where the hell did you get such an idea?"

"From Meredith," she replied, stunning him again.

"Meredith?"

"Yes!"

"Meredith told you I'd slept with her?" His voice resonated with his startled disbelief.

Her glare said she'd never hated anyone more than she hated him now. "No," she spat. "She couldn't tell me. She never had the chance. But after she died, I read her diary. 'I've decided to take Reed's advice and keep my baby. Reed says I'll make a wonderful mother.'" The words brought silent tears and watching them slip down her cheeks, Reed felt as though they were being wrung out of his own heart. "The last entry in her diary explained how much she loved you. I couldn't believe how you'd betrayed us both. And I still can't." With that final declaration, her shoulders slumped and all of the rage seemed to drain out of her.

Reed, too, felt weakened by her confession, his arms and legs ached, as though he'd just run a marathon in a lead suit.

"I loved her, too," he admitted as he brought his hand to her face and with his thumb and forefinger tilted her chin so that her eyes were forced to meet his. "I loved Meredith like a *sister,* Tess. She was the little sister I never had. You knew that. And now you have to believe there was never anything more than that."

When he dropped his hand from her face, Tess still felt strangely bound where she stood, bound by the things he was saying that she longed to believe.

"Yes. I knew she was pregnant," he admitted. "She came to me when she found out. She hadn't even told Buddy yet—"

"Buddy?" Tess murmured. "Buddy Cooper?" Tess couldn't remember her sister ever having dated Buddy.

Reed nodded. "When Meredith finally got up the courage to tell him, he offered money for an abortion. She was devastated, of course. She'd been dreaming up all sorts of ideas about weddings and baby showers." He seemed for a moment to be lost in his thoughts. "Anyway, after some pretty long and tense discussions, Meredith decided to keep her baby.

She was planning to tell your parents while the three of them were on that trip to Chicago."

Tess felt thunderstruck. "I always wondered why she wanted to go with them that day." Their father's business had never been of the least interest to Meredith before. Then she had begged her parents to let her miss school so that she could go with them for a week to Chicago.

When Reed started talking again, his voice was low and sad. "It was only a one-night stand. At a party after the basketball team took state. Everyone was drinking, including Buddy and Meredith."

A spark of memory flared inside Tess. The whole town had celebrated the year Evergreen High had won the state basketball championship. It had been Meredith's junior year—her last year, as it turned out.

Reed stood silently watching her, waiting for a judgment she wasn't yet prepared to make. Digesting the things he'd said would take time. But the dark, hard look in his eyes told her his pride wouldn't allow him to wait long. He'd finished explaining all he was prepared to explain. He'd never beg her to believe him. She knew him well enough to know that he'd bent as far as he could without breaking.

"It's almost noon," he said without looking at his watch. "I'll be leaving for Bodden Town in fifteen minutes." His voice was resolute. "If you want to come with me, we'll leave the bike here and take the Jeep. If you decide to go your own way, I'll take the bike and you can drive the Jeep back to Georgetown. Go to the police, go back to the hotel, go wherever you think you need to go and do whatever you need to do. But if I leave here alone, Tess, I won't be coming back. I hurt you and I'm sorry. But I wasn't the father of Meredith's child. Granted, I'm a bastard. I was a gutless wonder to run out on you that way. But not even I would stoop so low as to sleep with your little sister."

He'd started to walk away when he turned and added a somber, "Whatever else you think about me, believe me when I tell you that I still plan to do everything I can to find Selena and bring her back to the States safely. Even if it weren't my job, I figure I owe you that much." His promise was sealed with a final searing gaze that burned straight through to her heart.

Watching him walk away, a war waged inside Tess, a battle between the things he'd said and the things she'd believed to be reality for so long.

Oblivious to the gentle tide swirling around her feet and the warm breeze stirring her hair, Tess began to walk along the shore in the opposite direction. Absorbed in her thoughts of the past, she forced herself to remember anything and everything about the time just before her family was so abruptly and cruelly taken from her.

"Buddy Cooper," she whispered. Captain of the basketball team. Debate team leader. Tall, blond, confident. Yes, she remembered him now as clearly as if he stood before her.

Meredith had a crush on him—as she had at one time or another on most of the members of the basketball team that year. It was the year after Tess's high school graduation, and she remembered feeling a bit removed from all the excitement; her plans for the future with Reed occupied most of her time.

But even Tess had had to admit that the basketball team that year was special. The whole team was loaded with talent and a limitless belief in what they could achieve together. By the end of the season, they'd won the league championship and advanced to the state finals.

Half the town of Evergreen followed the team bus down the mountain to the tournament in Denver that spring. Meredith had ridden with a carload of her friends and Tess remembered her calling home that first night, wildly excited, after the team had won its semifinal game.

Against their father's wishes, their mother had agreed to let Meredith stay the night in Denver so that she wouldn't miss the state-championship game scheduled for the next day. The team had won and the celebrating had gone on all night.

And now, suddenly, all these years later, the impossible seemed possible. The words in the diary took on a different meaning. Reed had been a good friend. A friend to Meredith when she'd needed him most, someone to whom she'd confided and cried. A good friend. Nothing more.

Tess stopped, turned around and looked back, realizing with a shock that she could no longer see the bungalow in the distance. The beach had narrowed to a rocky strip and the hills that had seemed so far in the distance this morning now loomed right next to her.

How far had she walked? How long had she been thinking and sifting the past for the truth? She had no doubt that Reed would do exactly as he'd said he'd do—he would leave without her and never come back.

Suddenly the wasted years behind them seemed insignificant when compared to the future she'd almost squandered. And before another second of that future could be wasted, Tess started running.

Chapter Thirteen

The blow came from behind, knocking her to her knees and stunning her with the intense pain. Rough hands jerked her to her feet, and she fought to maintain consciousness, to make her legs move, to fight, scream, escape.

When she opened her mouth, an oily-smelling rag was tied over it. And when she tried to run, her feet were kicked out from under her. This time she fell forward and her arms were jerked behind her and bound with something tight and unrelenting that bit into her wrists when she struggled to free herself.

A man's voice behind her ordered, "Get up."

She struggled to her feet, a swarm of dizziness like a horde of angry insects stealing her equilibrium and making her stumble. Rough hands dragged her by the bonds that bound her wrists. Her knees were scraped and burning and her elbows were skinned and stinging. To keep her arms from breaking, she knew she had to try again to stand.

At last, she was on her feet, though wobbling. "This way," the voice commanded, with another vicious jerk. Tess had never had a concussion before, but she guessed she had one now. Her vision was blurred and the pain behind her eyes was like none she'd ever experienced before.

The sounds of the ocean were muted. She felt as though she'd just emerged from a swimming pool and her ears were still filled with water. The world swam before her eyes and no matter how hard she blinked, she couldn't seem to focus. Despite her blurry vision, she didn't need to see to know the man behind her was all too real. She could feel his sharp prodding whenever she stumbled.

She tried to scream, but the dirty rag tied across her mouth only gagged her. As she walked, her head throbbed and her heart ached. Selena's abductors now had another hostage, another victim. *Reed!* her mind cried. *Oh, Reed, please help me.* If only she hadn't left him. If only she'd trusted him, tried to believe in him.

Desperation gave way to full-scale panic and she swung around to lunge at her tormentor, only to find herself shoved backward again, and the whole painful process of trying to get to her feet started all over.

In this confused state, she had no idea in what direction she was headed, where she was being taken or how far she had to go.

Fifteen minutes, Reed had said and the sound of an engine in the distance triggered an inner voice that cried, "Time's up."

REED KILLED TIME by tinkering with the generator. He'd coaxed the motor to life twice but, despite its mighty roar, he couldn't keep it running for more than a few minutes before it choked and died. He told himself that whether he could get the machine running or not was pointless, since neither he nor Tess would be staying another night in the bungalow.

But he'd needed something to keep him busy, something onto which he could pour his frustrations. "Fifteen minutes, hell," he grumbled to himself as he worked. What kind of damn fool was he to have given her such a stupid ultimatum?

Tess Elliot was the kind of woman any man would wait for, no matter how long it took her to come back to him. She was as bright as she was beautiful, as sexy and savvy as any woman he'd ever known. A potent combination of spirit and tenderness he knew he'd regret losing for the rest of his life.

But his pride would force him to leave eventually; he knew himself well enough to realize that. When he did, he'd focus all his energies on finding Selena and getting her back to the States. He promised Tess he'd help her cousin and this was one promise he meant to keep. But his heart would always be with Tess, no matter where he went, what he did, or how much time passed.

Soon his silly fifteen minutes had stretched into an hour, and still he waited.

THE SMALL CAVE into which she was being forced was halfway up a steep trail, littered with sharp rocks and prickly vegetation. Tess's feet were sore and scraped by the time she was shoved into the dark cavern, through an opening so small she had to duck to keep from hitting her head. The day had turned hot and muggy and the cave was like an airless oven.

Her captor, who had taken pains to remain behind her all the way up the trail, seemed suddenly unconcerned that she should see him.

He was tall—taller than Reed, she guessed. Six-two, at least. His skin was the color of pale chocolate and his eyes were a pale gray. To Davey, they must have seemed silver, Tess reminded herself grimly.

The khaki shirt her abductor wore stuck to his back and his face was streaked with sweat. He wore tattered shorts and filthy tennis shoes and by the looks of his red-rimmed eyes, frazzled hair and beard stubble, he hadn't slept for at least a day.

Tess sat cross-legged against the wall of the cavern into which he'd forced her. She trembled, more frightened than she'd ever been, and more desperate. She had to find a way out, her mind screamed. She couldn't die alone in this wretched place with this horrid man. But how? How could she escape? The rope that held her hands was tied impossibly tight and her captor's cruelty had been well demonstrated on the gruelling trek to the cave.

She had only two choices, she told herself. Behind her, the back of the cave narrowed and disappeared into an ominous abyss that could have extended ten feet or ten miles as far as Tess could tell. In front of her, blocking the narrow opening was the man who'd attacked her, terrorized her and for all she knew tried to murder her last night.

The hopelessness of her situation caused her stomach to roil in protest. The pervasive smell of rotting vegetation and the taste of oil from the rag in her mouth didn't help matters.

Her captor, perched on his haunches just inside the narrow opening, stared out at the water. He startled her when he spoke. "You will notice that we are above a small bay, Miss Elliot. We call it Jack's Bay, but you will not find it named on any map. The water in Jack's Bay is very deep, very unsuitable for snorkeling but very good for deep dives." In the casual, yet impeccable English of the islands, he imparted the information in a soft, polite manner that startled her almost as much as his calling her by name.

"Fishermen favor this inlet in the spring, but this time of year the waters are left mostly undisturbed. Jack's Bay is very isolated. No one comes into this bay for months at a time."

He shocked her again when he unsheathed a sleek, narrow-bladed boning knife from the leather holster he wore strapped to the outside of his long, rangy leg and started toward her.

Tess shrank back against the cave wall, her eyes bulging. Her heart drummed so hard her chest hurt, but nothing else moved. Even the breath in her lungs froze when he brought the tip of the knife slowly to her throat and skimmed the deadly steel along her skin with a touch just light enough not to penetrate.

With the tip poised at the hollow of her throat, he leaned close. His breath was hot and sour against her face. "I have no wish to harm you, Miss Elliot," he said in a low ominous tone. "I am merely a courier. I am going to remove the gag, but if you scream when I do, I will slit your throat." He paused, letting the impact of his simple, deadly warning settle over her. "Do you understand?"

She could only blink her acceptance of his terrifying terms. With the cold steel still at her throat, she dared not make another move.

"I am glad you understand. This is very good. It is in your best interests to allow me to do my job." Then, with a lightning-fast flick of his wrist, he sliced the rag and it fell to her lap.

"Better?"

The knife was at her throat once more, but she nodded. "Y-yes," she stammered. "Thank you."

His smile was a sneer that stretched his pale lips over crooked and discolored teeth. "Tonight you will go down to Jack's Bay. At midnight a boat will come for you. If you are not there at midnight, the boat will not wait. If you are not alone, the boat will not dock."

"Selena," she gasped. "Will she—" Her question died on her lips when he pricked her with the knife just beneath her chin. She felt the pressure before she felt the pain and the warm trickle of blood sliding down her throat.

"Do not ask questions, Miss Elliot. Be assured I have no answers for you. I am merely a messenger. Do you understand?"

Again, she could only stare, more terrified than she'd have believed it possible to be without dying of fright. To move, even to breathe, would cause the knife to slice into her skin again, and his last painful warning had made her a believer in his indifference to her terror.

"You will bring with you what has been requested. Remember to come alone."

The journal! her mind shrieked. "B-but I—" He threatened her again with the knife.

"Please, Miss Elliot. I have not been paid to kill you and I have no wish to do so," he said quietly, but she couldn't have been more terrified if he'd shouted. His cold-blooded, dispassionate tone told her that her life meant nothing to him, that killing her would be easy, if inconvenient.

He edged away from her, the knife still steady in his long, thin fingers. "I am merely a messenger," he reiterated.

You're a murderer! she thought, remembering the devastation of the explosion at Davey's bar last night.

"You are free to go now," he said from the cave's entrance. "But know this, Miss Elliot, I have many friends on the island, many relatives. If you go to the police, I will kill you. If you tell anyone about me or the message I have delivered to you, I will kill you. I will find you wherever you are and I will use this knife to kill you. Do you understand, Miss Elliot?"

His tone hadn't wavered, hadn't varied a single note in its maddening formality. He could have been the desk clerk at West Palm, except for his eyes, which were as cold as ice.

"I will be behind you on the trail and I'll be watching you on the beach. Do not cry out for help. I was raised in these hills and I know them as well as I know my own face. Do not turn around to look for me. You will not see me. But be assured, Miss Elliot, that I will see you, and be assured that my knife will find you wherever you go."

He edged out of the cave with the stealth of an animal, and for one astonishing moment, Tess wondered if this was all just a horrible nightmare, and the silver-eyed monster had been conjured up from her own imagination.

But the rope that held her was real, as was the thin trickle of blood that seeped down her neck. "My hands—" she blurted, "they're still tied. Please, won't you at least . . ."

But it was too late; he was gone.

AT FIRST she was too terrified and hysterical to move. She could still feel the cold steel at her throat, still hear the silver-eyed man's warning as it reverberated through her mind like an echo.

What if, even now, he was waiting for her just outside the cave?

He'd said he would be watching. He'd said he would find her, that his knife would find her no matter where she went.

Inside the cave, the temperature had to be in the upper nineties and yet Tess had to clench her teeth to keep them from chattering. How long she crouched there, frozen by fear, paralyzed by the unbelievable events that had just occurred, she couldn't guess. But slowly and without fanfare, she felt her inner strength coming back to her, the strength that had seen her down the side of mountains that would have made a mountain goat dizzy and that had helped her go on living when there hadn't been anyone left to live for.

"Let's go, Tess," a ragged whisper she barely recognized as her own ordered. *So he scared the hell out of you? All right. Haven't you been afraid before and*

*survived? He's gone now and you've got two good legs
to walk out of here on. So get up. Get out. Get going.*

Tess inched her way to the cave opening and peered
out. True to his word, her captor was nowhere to be
seen.

From this lofty vantage point she could see a narrow strip of beach and a concrete pier that ran almost
a hundred feet out into the bay. She would use the pier
as a marker tonight, she told herself, clinging to the
hope that she would live long enough to make the
rendezvous and free Selena.

Tess stared down at the water. The steep cliffs that
ringed the bay cast the deep water in shadows, making it appear alternately black and green as it moved
with the tide. Beyond lay a sunlit sea of sparkling
white and sky blue, a startling contrast, making the
dark, shadowy waters of the inlet seem all the more
ominous.

Tess stared out at the isolated cove, and wondered
how the bay would look in the moonlight. She would
find out soon enough, she told herself as she focused
her attention on freeing her hands.

The unrelenting heat and the ropes that restricted
circulation were causing her wrists to swell and ache.
Stumbling out of the cave, Tess's eyes scanned the
ground and the sides of the cave entrance for something with which to sever the ropes at her wrists.

The rough edge of a jutting boulder captured her
attention and she backed up to it and began working

the cords across the jagged edge. Wriggling and twisting her hands, she helped the process along, and by the time her bonds finally fell away, her hands were not only tingling from the lack of blood supply, but scraped and raw, as well.

With her hands free, Tess felt better, more able to negotiate the rocky path of the steep incline. Although the soles and sides of her feet were tender and swollen, she moved quickly, the eerie sensation of silver eyes boring into her back, propelling her along the trail.

Tess spun around, her heart in her throat, to see nothing more threatening than a startled bird taking flight. Although she couldn't see him, Tess knew the man with the silver eyes and the long knife was out there, watching.

REED THREW the rusty wrench into the sand and swore, glanced at his watch for the hundredth time and released an exasperated sigh. "To hell with it," he grumbled. She wasn't coming back and the longer he kidded himself, the longer it would take him to find the silver-eyed messenger, track down Selena Elliot and get the hell off this godforsaken island.

As he swung his leg over the bike and stomped the starter to life, he repressed the urge to ride down the beach in search of Tess.

But why prolong the torture for both of them? he asked himself. She was better off without him; hadn't he always known that? And now, evidently she knew it, as well.

WHEN TESS finally reached the beach, the cool and wet sand felt soothing to her battered feet. She stooped to bathe the crusted blood from her neck, and the salt water stung the spot beneath her chin that had been nicked by the silver-eyed man's knife.

She looked around to see that the hills had fallen gradually away behind her and she recognized the familiar stretch of beach leading to the bungalow. In the distance she saw the roof of the little beach house and she quickened her pace, shoving aside the ache in her heart that reminded her that he wouldn't be there when she arrived.

In the distance, Tess saw a half a dozen boats drifting aimlessly on the shimmering sea. The impulse to call out to the fishermen and divers who manned those vessels was strong. But what could they do? What could anyone do? Her only bargaining tool, Selena's notebook, was gone, and for all she knew, Selena could already be dead. Her breath came in gasps past a searing lump in her throat. Despite all the horrible realities that faced her, the fact remained that tonight at midnight she'd be standing on the shore at Jack's Bay, still hoping for a miracle.

ONCE SHE WAS INSIDE the beach house again, the emptiness felt even more oppressive than it had this morning. In the bathroom, Tess assessed the damage to her aching body. A lump the size of a small egg had swelled at the back of her head, but the cut under her chin wasn't deep and it was no longer bleeding.

While dabbing at the back of her head with a cold, wet washcloth, she discovered a bottle of aspirin and a box of bandages in the medicine cabinet. After swallowing three pills with a handful of water, she locked the front door, closed the windows and stripped off all her clothes.

The smell of the cave and the horrible man who'd abducted her seemed to cling to every pore, making her feel filthy and violated. In the shower, the cool water revived her as she lathered and rinsed for a full five minutes.

When she'd dried she regretted having to put her dirty clothes back on, but the bag with all her belongings was long gone, discarded, she supposed, by the so-called messenger. After she'd dressed, she pasted a Band-Aid under her chin and half a dozen smaller ones on her feet, gingerly slipped on her canvas sneakers and headed for the Jeep.

Outside, the sun was high and the air was hot and muggy. Out of habit, Tess glanced down at her wrist to realize for the first time that her watch had been lost in the scuffle with her abductor. Tess clutched the keys to the Jeep in her hand as she hurried along the deserted beach toward the dead end where the vehicle was parked. That the keys hadn't been lost during her ordeal was nothing short of a miracle.

When Tess's eager eyes caught sight of the Jeep parked in the distance, a single thought possessed her mind: she had to find Reed McKenna, and find him fast.

SHE BARELY suppressed a scream when she saw that the Jeep's tires had been slashed. A picture of a long, thin boning knife formed in her mind and she knew instantly who had done the cutting. The thought that he might be watching her even now raised goose bumps on her flesh and, despite the tender condition of her feet, she began to run toward the main road.

She'd walked and run almost a mile when a man and a woman in a dusty foreign car picked her up on the road and drove her the rest of the way to Bodden Town, dropping her at the gas station at the edge of the village.

Three men who looked as though they might be natives of the island lounged beneath a canopy and sipped Cokes from sweating bottles. When one of them smiled at her, Tess realized she'd been staring, thinking how wonderful a cold soda would taste right now. But that kind of creature comfort would have to wait, she told herself. Right now, all she could allow herself to think about was finding Reed.

She acknowledged the trio sitting in the shade with what she hoped was a confident nod, before starting off toward the center of town. A sprinkling of gift shops and dive shops were mixed among the inevitable bars and open-air cafés.

For what seemed like hours, Tess walked in and out of curio shops, her eyes darting and nervous as she scanned the faces of the tourists and natives she encountered on the sidewalk. The man with the silver eyes had said he had many friends, many relatives and that warning came back to haunt Tess with her every move.

At the end of the street, Tess's heart was heavy as she crossed and started back up the other side. She'd hoped by now in a town this small to have literally tripped over Reed.

Out of the corner of her eye she noticed a grass hut that rented snorkeling gear and catamarans and she walked toward it. The ubiquitous reggae music drifted out of a massive boom box sitting on the end of the open-air bar next door.

When she reached the rental shack and spotted a black motorcycle parked between the two businesses, her heart lurched and she crossed the sandy lot quickly, straining to get a better look at the small group of five or six people gathered around the dive shop. Disappointed not to see Reed among them, Tess turned her attention on the bar.

Beneath the large thatched roof the temperature was at least ten degrees cooler and a breeze off the water played between the tables. The bar was crowded with scantily clad tourists and weathered beachcombers sipping rum punch and nibbling shrimp from large wooden bowls.

A strikingly beautiful young woman with skin the color of burnished gold and black hair hanging past her waist threaded her way effortlessly through the crowd and among the tables, taking orders. Tess noticed by the way the waitress dealt with the male customers that the young woman was a born flirt. If a man as strikingly sexy as Reed McKenna had been here today, this beautiful young woman would remember.

Tess hung back, waiting for the girl to return to the bar and place her orders. As soon as she did, Tess moved up beside her. As she described Reed to the waitress, the young woman smiled. "Ah, yes," she said, nodding. Her black hair shimmered and swayed like a silken veil. "I do remember the man you described. Such a good-looking American. Yes, he was here earlier."

The girl reached for her tray and Tess followed her. "He didn't mention where he was going, did he?" Tess didn't really expect that he had, so when the young woman nodded and said, "Yes, he asked for directions to Orman's Boat Rentals," Tess found herself speechless.

Half a mile south of the bar, true to the young waitress's directions, the sandy knoll gave way to a narrow strip of beach. Tethered along the length of a wooden dock were boats of all descriptions. At the edge of the beach, beneath a cluster of palms, stood the plywood shack the waitress had described. The shack was deserted, but behind the ramshackle structure a tall, thin, gray-haired man was shoving a boat filled with noisy teenagers away from the dock.

The man turned around and spotted Tess as the outboard engine roared to life and the boat sped out into the turquoise sea. Hurrying down the wooden sidewalk that led to the dock, Tess met the proprietor halfway.

As they walked back to the makeshift office, she asked about Reed, describing him in detail.

"Yeah, he's been here. Didn't rent nothin', though. Asked a lot of questions and then went about his business."

Tess's spirits plummeted.

"You need a boat, miss? You won't find better rates on the island," he promised.

She shook her head, feeling almost too disappointed to speak. "I wonder, could you tell me how long ago my friend was here? It's very important that I find him."

The old man, clad only in a pair of baggy black shorts with skin as leathery and tanned as the sandals he wore, rubbed his head and thought. "Well, I don't exactly know. But I think I can figure it out."

She followed him as he walked up the wooden steps to the rental shack and watched him flip open a notebook lying on the counter. "He was here just after I rented that pontoon rig...let's see...yeah, seems like I was just getting them folks wrapped up when he came by. Now let's see, what time was that? Seems like it was three, but it coulda been closer to three-thirty..."

As his clawlike finger skimmed the entries in the book, Tess stopped hearing his muttering, her attention completely distracted by the old man's logbook, with its tight rows of numbers and dates.

The idea formed quickly and she wondered why it hadn't occurred to her sooner. If she could somehow duplicate Selena's journal, she wouldn't have to face her cousins' abductors empty-handed. She'd be taking a desperate risk, but what choice did she have?

If the men holding Selena were merely hired thugs, as Reed had suggested, they wouldn't know one set of figures from another. It was worth a try, she decided. If nothing else, at least it would buy precious time. And right now, with the shadows of the giant palms already beginning to lengthen, time was a precious commodity.

If she'd found Reed, or if she'd had any money of her own, she would never have contemplated stealing Orman's logbook. As it was, the only question left now was how to take it without getting caught.

The answer came almost immediately in the form of a vanload of tourists. Orman was overjoyed at the sight of them pulling up to his shack. "Excuse me," he said as he left the shack to greet them, "but these

folks reserved a fishing rig for this evening and I need
to help them get aboard.''

Two more cars pulled up behind the van and Tess
knew it was now or never. With one eye on Orman and
the other on the logbook, she picked it up, slid it under her blouse and started walking quickly back in the
direction of the bar.

And when the hand clamped over her shoulder, she
thought her heart would stop.

Chapter Fourteen

"Excuse me, but does Mr. Orman know you're borrowing his logbook?" The large hand planted authoritatively on her shoulder belonged to a tall, sandy-haired American with startling blue eyes and a firm, no-nonsense mouth.

"Well, I—I... You see, that is..." Tess stammered as her mind raced to find a plausible excuse.

"Please come with me, Miss Elliot."

If she'd been shocked by his sudden appearance, she was even more shocked by the fact that he knew her name. Instinctively she drew back.

"Who are you?" she demanded, clutching the logbook protectively to her chest.

He stared at her, his face passive, but at the same time he slipped his arm around her waist and pulled her with him toward a small foreign car parked behind the van. "I wouldn't cause a scene if I were you," he warned in a low voice. "The Bodden Town jail is a nasty place for someone as lovely as you to have to spend the night."

Tess dug in her heels, but he continued to pull her forward with enough muscle to convince her that he wouldn't let her go without a full-fledged fight.

"Come on, Tess," he urged her. "I'm here to help."

She looked up at him and a vague recognition dawned. "I know you—that is, I've seen you before, haven't I?"

He smiled. "You're very observant."

"Where?"

"At the hotel. I was staying at West Palm when you were. In fact, I was only there because you were, or more correctly, because that's where your cousin was staying."

"Selena!" she blurted, struggling to break free of his grip. "You have Selena!"

"No," he said firmly. "But I wish I did. Now get in the car, Tess. And I'll tell you how your government is prepared to help you."

Tess couldn't have been more surprised if the man sitting next to her in the rental car had said he was King Neptune, just arrived from Atlantis. As it was, her mouth fell open and she moved like a sleepwalker as he opened the car door and ushered her inside.

As her mind reeled with a thousand questions, he produced a small leather case. With a flick of his wrist it opened to reveal a silver badge and an official picture, identifying him as Nicholas Talbot, special agent, United States Government.

REED'S HUNCHES had paid off. At the open-air market in town he'd found lots of friendly locals who'd directed him to the home of the young man they referred to as "Paolo." Whether it was his first name or his last, Reed couldn't be sure, and at the moment didn't care. But that Paolo was widely known and widely disrespected had been clear.

"That would be him," an elderly woman had said, nodding her gray head as she arranged colorful straw hats in her shop. "He's a curse on his mother," she'd declared. "He's in jail more than he's at that rat's nest he calls home. And while his father is out fishing, he's in Georgetown gambling away the family's money."

Another local had confirmed the old woman's opinion of Paolo, remarking that as far as he knew, the best place to find Paolo was either in jail or just getting out. But the information that Reed found most interesting was the fact that Paolo had been seen lately driving a secondhand limousine.

After calling West Palm to check in with Gertie and Jake, Reed headed out to confront Paolo. Armed with a pocketful of Cayman money and the impression that Paolo would do anything for a fast buck, Reed rode the motorcycle to the outskirts of town where the dusty side road headed north.

Paolo's shack, if Reed had found the right one, was a grass hut with trash piled outside the front door almost to the thatched roof.

"Charming," he muttered to himself as he got off the bike and stood staring at the squalor.

A rusted out '55 Chevy, missing a hood and an engine, sat like a hulking steel corpse on blocks in the front yard. Approaching the house cautiously, Reed gambled that the absence of a roadworthy vehicle meant Paolo was not at home.

On the south side of the house a pathetic greyhound was tethered to a post by a heavy rope. A filthy bowl, black with flies and dry as dust, was just beyond his reach. The dog was obviously too weak to bark and merely lifted his head and watched with pitiful eyes as Reed approached the hut.

The front door, if it could be called that, had no knob and no lock and was attached to a makeshift frame by two leather hinges. Reed drew his gun and edged inside to find a sweltering, cockroach-infested mess.

Once inside, Reed observed the evidence of Paolo's drug use scattered everywhere. And as if he needed more evidence to know that Paolo lived on the edge, Reed saw through the open back door that a half acre of marijuana plants swayed in the breeze.

The smell of rotting garbage and the heat drove Reed back to the door, but not before his eyes landed on something shiny lying on the table at one end of the room.

Holstering his gun, he walked over and picked up a lady's watch. Instantly he recognized it as Tess's. She'd been wearing it last night when they arrived at the bungalow and, seeing it here in now, in the middle of this snake's den, caused his stomach to clench. His pulse pounded in his ears and something close to panic seized his heart.

Picking up the watch, he slipped it into his pocket as his eyes scanned the room and he saw her bag with her clothes spilling out on the floor in front of a ragged couch. Again, he felt a searing reaction in his gut.

When he bent down to pick the bag up, he heard a strange whizzing noise pass his ear and glanced up in time to see Paolo's knife stab into the wall behind him.

Raw, animal anger propelled him toward the tall, thin, silver-eyed man standing in the doorway. When Reed hit him, Paolo flew backward out the door. Reed was over the strange-looking man in a heartbeat. Grabbing Paolo's shirt, he dragged the thief to his feet and back into the house.

"Where did you get this?" he growled, shoving him toward the bag of Tess's clothing.

"I found it." As he lied, the expression in his strange eyes never changed and Reed knew the man would not be easily intimidated.

"And this?" Reed pulled Tess's watch from his pocket. "I suppose you found it, as well?"

The young man was still doubled over, but suddenly and without warning he spun around and lunged at Reed headfirst, with a strength that was surprising. Reed reached for his gun, but a sudden, sharp pain in his left side took his breath away and rendered him momentarily defenseless.

Reflexively, his fist shot up, catching Paolo squarely beneath the chin, to send him sprawling backward across the room, where his dark head made contact with the wall with a sickening thud.

With the thug off his back, Reed glanced down to see the handle of a small stiletto sticking out of his side. With the roar of a wounded grizzly he jerked the two-inch blade from his flesh and clamped his hand over the oozing wound.

Stumbling across the rancid-smelling room, his hand pressed to the stab wound, he felt the blood seeping between his fingers and staining his shirt. Reed pulled his gun and sank down beside the half-conscious young man on the floor.

"Where is...she?" he gasped, pressing the gun to Paolo's dark temple with convincing force.

The young man shook his head and muttered something unintelligible.

Reed pulled back the hammer, even as the world tilted beneath him. "I'll count to three...before I...pull the...trigger. F-feel free...to stop me at any...time." Every word cost him, but then again he only needed to say three more, Reed told himself. "One, two..."

ONE LOOK at the badge and the rush of relief that flooded Tess made her feel weak. "You'll never know how glad I am to see you," she blurted.

"I'm glad to see you, as well, Miss Elliot," the agent admitted. "You gave me quite a scare last night when I lost track of you at the bar outside Georgetown."

"You were following me?" This was incredible, right out of one of the novels on the shelves of her bookstore back home.

Agent Talbot nodded, his expression grim. "We've known where you were from the day your cousin disappeared."

She shouldn't have been surprised; of course Reed would have been in contact with his agency. But why, she wondered, had he not told her that there were other agents in Grand Cayman? Why the "us against the world" act?

"Do you know where my cousin is, Agent Talbot?"

He stared at her intently before he shook his head, his face an unreadable mask that Tess found herself instantly and deeply resenting.

"No, I'm sorry. I'm afraid I don't know where Selena is, but as you might imagine the agency is very anxious to find her."

He pulled the car into a parking lot south of Bodden Town overlooking a public beach. As they drove in, carloads of sun-worshippers were pulling out. The heavy layer of clouds and a brisk wind had risen, bringing in cooler air and the promise of rain.

Tess and Agent Talbot sat in his rental car with the windows rolled down.

"Miss Elliot, has your cousin contacted you?"

"My cousin?" Tess blurted. "Don't you mean my cousin's abductors?"

"Why, yes. Yes, of course, that's what I meant. The kidnappers . . . have they contacted you?"

A vague alarm began to sound at the back of Tess's mind. "Wait a minute," she said her hand on the door. "Where's McKenna? Why don't you know more about what's been happening?"

He smile was almost a sneer. "I'm sure *you* would know more about Reed McKenna's whereabouts than I, Miss Elliot."

Something was definitely wrong here, Tess told herself. "I haven't spoken with Reed since this morning," she explained. "I guess I just assumed he would have tried to contact you."

The smile again, but this time insultingly patronizing. "Why would you think McKenna would contact me? After all, he hasn't been a part of the agency for almost four years."

Whatever he said after that went unheard as Tess tried to understand why Reed McKenna had been lying to her from the moment he'd appeared at her door the night of Selena's disappearance.

REED DIDN'T KNOW what kind of damage the small, sharp stiletto had done to his body, but he knew he couldn't risk trying to keep a bike upright on the rutted dirt road back to Bodden Town.

"Get up," he ordered the young man sitting on the floor opposite him.

With the gun at his back, Reed ordered Paolo into the front yard. After fumbling for a moment, he managed to remove the rope from around the greyhound's neck. Finally freed, the dog stumbled into the shade beneath the wrecked car and collapsed with an exhausted sigh.

With the gun cocked and aimed at Paolo's heart, Reed moved toward him with the rope. When the young man realized what Reed meant to do he began backing away, his hands raised. "No. No. You can't do this to me."

Paolo fell to his knees. "Please, I'll do anything."

"Tell me where she is," Reed growled.

"I don't know."

Reed drew the hammer back on his gun and aimed the barrel at Paolo's head.

"Okay, okay, I was with her—yes. B-but I didn't hurt her. She's all right."

Reed shoved the young man face-first into the dirt and tied his hands and feet behind him. "She'd better be, you son of a bitch, or you'll wish you'd never seen my face. Now keep talking until I tell you to stop."

Paolo told Reed about the rendezvous, about Jack's Bay and about the message he was supposed to have delivered to Tess at The Dive last night.

"But you decided to blow the place up instead, right?"

"I know nothing of the explosion," Paolo insisted. "I was only paid to deliver the message for Miss Elliot to be at Jack's Bay tonight at midnight."

"Who paid you?" Reed demanded to know.

"I don't know."

Reed looped the remaining length of rope around his neck and jerked it tight. "Who?" he shouted. "Who paid you?"

"I—I don't know," Paolo gasped. "I was given my orders by phone and the money was left in the cave above Jack's Bay. I never saw the man who left it."

Reed had dealt with liars long enough to know when he was hearing the truth, even from a practiced liar like the one who lay facedown in the dirt in front of him. With another knot, Reed effectively harnessed Paolo to the sturdy stake on which the dog had been tied.

"When I get back to Bodden Town, I'll send the local police out to water and feed you," Reed said, his voice caustic with the contempt he felt for Paolo. "Which is a hell of a lot more than you did for that poor animal. And more than you deserve."

After filling the cleanest bowl he could find with water from a hand pump inside the hut and leaving it for the dog, Reed found the keys to Paolo's limousine and climbed behind the wheel. His wound had stopped bleeding, but it had begun to throb, keeping time with the pounding in his head.

Before he drove away, he took careful aim and, with two shots, flattened the tires on the motorcycle. If old silver-eyes somehow managed to work his way free before the police arrived, Reed had no desire to give him an easy means of escape. The man was hate filled and dangerous. He had been beaten and humiliated and if he managed to get lose he would be bent on revenge. Because of the confession Reed had extracted from him at gunpoint, Paolo would know exactly where to find him tonight at midnight.

AFTER QUESTIONING her for over three hours, Agent Talbot offered to drive Tess back to West Palm. Since she hadn't told him about the rendezvous at Jack's Bay, she couldn't give him a good reason for wanting to remain in Bodden Town. Afraid if she pressed the issue she'd arouse his suspicions, Tess accepted his offer.

Sitting in his car outside the hotel, Tess thanked him for the lift and reached for the door, only to have him stop her.

"It was extremely foolish for you to think you could track down the man the bartender described," he admonished her. "I hope you realize now what a mistake that was."

Tess nodded, but the only thing she realized was that Nick Talbot was a condescending ass.

"Remember, if you think of anything you've forgotten, anything your cousin may have shared with you, anything at all that could help us find her, you must call me. I'm staying at the Georgetown Holiday Inn in room 612. Don't forget. I'm the federal authority in this case. I can't help you out of this mess if you won't confide in me, Miss Elliot. Do you understand?"

Tess muttered that she did and moments later stood on the sidewalk outside West Palm and watched the rental car pull away. She'd been relieved three hours ago to discover that Nick Talbot was a federal agent, but now, ironically, she was even more relieved to see him go.

On the way back to the hotel, he'd attempted to bring levity to what had ultimately been a grueling afternoon by handing her Orman's boat rental logbook and making her promise to send it back to the old man.

"Seriously, Tess," he'd said, staring at her like an overbearing father, "if the kidnappers contact you again, you must call me. You've interfered in a serious criminal matter. I only hope you haven't compromised the state's case entirely." He'd stared at her almost angrily. "Promise you'll go straight to the nearest phone and call me. No more cops and robbers with McKenna.''

Tess had agreed, knowing it was a promise she'd never keep. Her experience on the beach this morning had convinced her that the men who held Selena were deadly serious about killing her cousin if Tess did not comply exactly with their wishes. And her experience with Talbot had convinced her that he cared far more about the prosecution of Edward Morrell than saving Selena's life.

Despite his persistent questioning, Tess hadn't told Talbot everything. In order to justify her presence in Bodden Town she'd had to admit to what Davey had told them about the silver-eyed man. But every time she'd considered telling him about her ordeal in the cave or the rendezvous tonight, she remembered the deadly warning she'd received at knifepoint.

The more Nick Talbot had badgered her, the easier it had become to lie to him. His demeanor had been condescending and ultimately chauvinistic. In the end, those disagreeable traits had worked to Tess's advantage.

She'd convinced him, or at least she hoped she had, that if Selena's abductors contacted her again she'd be all too happy to turn the rescue of her cousin over to him.

What Nick Talbot had convinced her of was that he was a coldhearted, by-the-book cop who thought in terms of cases first and people later. Although she couldn't argue with a cop dedicated to duty, she'd be damned if she'd compromise her cousin's life just to help some ambitious federal agent earn a promotion.

But if she didn't feel she could trust Nick Talbot, a bona fide federal agent, what made her think Reed McKenna, bounty hunter, could be any more trustworthy? And why, despite everything Talbot had told her, did she long to feel Reed's arms around her again?

AFTER FEIGNING amazement and distress at the news of the damage done to her room while she'd been away for the night in Bodden Town, Tess had not only received an apology from the hotel management, but been given a complimentary room. Time seemed to stand still while she waited in the lobby while housekeeping prepared her new room, but at least she had time to phone the company that had issued her traveler's checks and report them stolen. She would have to stay long enough to check into the new room, she told herself, in case Talbot tried to reach her. At least from the privacy of a hotel room, she could make arrangements for a way back to Bodden Town, she told herself as she waited.

It was late, after nine when she finally opened the door to the room on the third floor. As she reached for the light switch, her every thought was focused on how to get back to Jack's Bay by midnight.

Nothing prepared her for the hand that came out of the darkness and clamped over her mouth, or the arm, as unrelenting as steel, that caught her around her waist and hauled her into the room and up against a rock-hard body in the darkness.

Chapter Fifteen

The door was kicked shut and adrenaline, like lightning, shot through Tess's veins, supplying her with a sudden burst of strength. She struggled, kicking and jabbing and flailing against the iron grip that held her.

"Tess! Tessa, be still."

At the sound of his smoky whisper, she stopped struggling immediately and all her fight dissolved into a maddening mix of anger and joy.

Reed! He'd come back. But damn it, he'd also nearly given her heart failure, not to mention the little matter of the charade he'd perpetrated for the past seventy-two hours, and the lies, that if he hadn't told outright, he hadn't gone out of his way to dispel, either.

Twisting around in his arms she stared into the familiar face, handsome even when shrouded in shadows. Not knowing whether to slap him or kiss him, she settled for scolding. "You scared the living hell out of me, McKenna," she informed him hotly before jerking out of his arms. When she twisted away from him to slap on the lights, she heard the breath go out of him in a ragged gasp.

His ghastly pallor shocked her. "What's the matter, Reed? Are you hurt?"

"I—I had a little accident," he muttered as he staggered to the bed. "A run-in with your friend from the beach." Blood was beginning to seep from his wound and Tess watched in horror as it formed a crimson circle on his shirt.

"We've got to call a doctor." She reached for the phone, but he grabbed her hand, stopping her.

"No, it's all right—really. I just...need to...lie down for a minute."

Against her better judgment she moved away from the phone and helped him lie back on the bed before she rushed into the bathroom, filled the plastic ice bucket with water and returned with a towel and washrag to inspect and clean his wound. He winced when she helped him out of his shirt and she suppressed a gasp when she saw the puncture wound in his side. "Reed, I don't know...it could be serious. I really think you need to see a doctor."

"Believe me, I couldn't have driven here if it had done any real damage," he assured her.

She cleaned the wound and realized he was right, that the blood seeping through his shirt had made the puncture seem deeper and more severe than it really was. But the depth and the severity didn't diminish the pain and she flinched every time he did.

Binding the wound would keep it from bleeding and might even ease the discomfort, Tess decided, and she proceeded to strip the pillowcases from pillows on the other bed, from which she fashioned bandages.

After the makeshift bandage was wrapped around his waist, Tess secured it with safety pins she found in a courtesy kit on the dresser.

"How did you know I'd come back to West Palm?" she asked as she worked over his wound.

"Well, as much as I'd like to tell you it was a work of brilliant detection, the real truth is I followed you."

"But how did you find me?"

"By accident," he admitted. "After a dismal attempt at first aid in the men's room at the Bodden Town gas station, I headed back to the beach house." Reed didn't tell her how the sight of the Jeep with its tires slashed reminded him that Paolo had been there and for a moment, imagining the wretched drug user with Tess, Reed had felt capable of cold-blooded murder.

"I didn't know if you'd found a ride back to Bodden Town or if you were still at the beach house," he explained. "But I knew that no matter what had transpired between us earlier, you were as focused on finding the silver-eyed man as I was." Tess was smart, independent, savvy. Too smart and too damned independent to merely sit and wait for someone to rescue her. "I decided you'd have found a way back to Bodden Town, even if you had to walk."

He was pleased by the smile he brought to her face.

"Anyway, I was pulling the limo onto the highway to double back to find you when I saw you and Talbot drive by."

Her eyes held his for a meaningful moment and he knew she was fully aware that he was not a federal agent. "Must have been a shock to see us together," she noted dryly.

He nodded and closed his eyes.

Tess watched him wince and was dismayed to see his face was still almost as pale as the pillowcase beneath his cap of wavy, black hair.

"How about a beer?"

He smiled and she reached for the phone.

"God, I could sure use a smoke."

"No way, McKenna," she informed him, as she sat back down on the edge of the bed beside him. "I didn't spend all this time saving your life just to have you turn around and throw it away."

When room service answered, she ordered dinner for both of them and when she hung up the phone she said, "I've got to be back at Jack's Bay in less than two hours."

Reed swung his legs over the side of the bed and sat up. "We'll have to start back soon. But I think it would be a good idea if we found a different car. That limo is a rolling wreck and I pushed it pretty hard when I saw you and Talbot. Jesus, I hope you didn't tell him anything.''

"I didn't," she snapped. "But since you've brought up the subject of confessions, why the hell did you tell me you were a cop?''

One black brow arched indignantly. "*You* said I was a cop, remember?''

"And you didn't bother to set me straight.''

He frowned. "No. I guess I didn't.''

She turned away from him to stare out at the rain that had begun to pepper the glass doors. Neither of them spoke for a long moment until finally Tess whispered, "We can't make it, Reed, can we? Our history is too full of lies and mistrust.''

He came around behind her and his reflection stared at her from the glass. "I wasn't the father of Meredith's child.''

She nodded and managed a weak, "I believe you.''

"And when I walked out on you all those years ago, I thought I was doing you a favor, saving you from a man who could never be the kind of husband you deserved.''

"I believe that, too. Now.''

He placed both hands on her shoulders and turned her gently around to face him. "Then believe this, Tessa. I love you. I always have. I need you. I always have.''

She looked deep into his eyes and knew every word he said was true.

"What else is there, Tessa? What more do we need?"

"Trust," she whispered. "Simple trust." She searched his face, looking for the answers that would banish her doubts and give them a new beginning. If she had the sense God gave a fish, she would just walk away, she told herself, wash her hands of this man with the troubled past and the uncertain future. He'd said it himself: it was a mistake to trust him. He got what he wanted by any means. He'd lived a life of hardship and become a hard man.

"Who are you, Reed?" she whispered. "The tender, gentle man who made love to me last night, or the tough, streetwise bounty hunter, the mercenary, who's out for no one but himself?"

He didn't reply, but the pain she saw flickering in his dark eyes squeezed her heart and every instinct told her to reach out to him. But a knock at the door stopped her; room service and the ticking clock stopped her, along with common sense and a survival instinct that she, too, had had to hone over the years.

They ate a silent meal together, perhaps the last meal they'd ever share before they went out into the rain together to look for the answers they both needed to find so desperately.

THEY decided on the way back to Bodden Town that Tess would meet the boat on the pier with the logbook she'd stolen from Orman's boat rental. Whether the abductors fell for the phony book determined what would happen next.

Reed figured that Paolo had been assigned to watch from the shore, to be sure Tess came alone. Now, thanks to the Bodden Town local constabulary, whom Reed had called with an anonymous report of Paolo's latest drug crop, Paolo was no longer a factor. Despite the bursts of pain from his wound, Reed felt fairly secure in his ability to back Tess up without interference. Now all they needed was a bit of luck.

"We should have time to launch the small boat from the beach house before they arrive," Reed said. Looking at his own watch reminded her that he still had hers in his pocket. A sentimental longing to hold on to something of hers kept him from returning it just yet.

"Try to remain on the shore or on the pier," he warned, outlining the details of his plan as she drove the small foreign car he'd hot-wired in the hotel parking lot. "If they force you to go aboard, I'll still be able to get to you by using the fishing boat, but it could definitely make things tougher."

"I'm so frightened," she admitted frankly. "I've never felt more afraid in my life."

"I'll be there," he promised, reaching for her hand across the darkness. And he meant it. He'd do everything humanly possible to protect her tonight. Tess's safety was his primary concern. Their future was still a dark uncertainty.

In the end, if Selena could not be convinced to come back to the States with him, he would have to play his trump card and reveal to Tess that all the doubts she still had about him were justified.

AN HOUR LATER they were on the beach outside of Bodden Town. Blessedly the rain had stopped, but the air was cold and the breeze was wet and chilling, and the moon played hide-and-seek behind a smattering of clouds left behind by the storm.

"How's your side?" Tess asked as they walked together back to the beach house.

By the pale moonlight reflected off the water, she saw him smile. "Not bad. You're a good nurse."

"When this is over I'm taking you to the hospital. I doubt you'll need stitches, but a tetanus shot wouldn't hurt."

He put his arm around her and hugged her. "I'm fine, Tessa. Let's just concentrate on getting through tonight alive and worry about patching me up later."

They hiked the rest of the way to the beach house and then launched the small fishing boat in the dark water and traveled back to Jack's Bay with the low hum of a trolling motor filling the silence between them. Even though they'd made good time, when they shoved the boat up on the narrow strip of sand that edged the dark waters of the bay they had less than ten minutes to spare.

Reed hauled the small craft up on the shore before turning to her. "This is it, Tessa."

She could only nod. The emotion clogging her throat made speech impossible.

Standing in the shadows, he touched her cheek, trying to memorize the feel of her. "I should have married you, my pretty Tessa," he declared in a smoky voice. "We would have made it, I know that now."

"I love you, Reed," she admitted, finding her voice shaky. "You warned me. I warned myself. I know I shouldn't, but I do."

They stood face-to-face, drinking in one last look. By the light of the moon Tess saw a tough, dangerous man in faded jeans and a black T-shirt with a gun holstered beneath his arm. He was pale, but the dark beard stubble that had risen during the day made him appear even more rugged, like the infamous pirates who had claimed this dangerous coast as their own.

And now this modern pirate had staked his claim on Tess's heart in exactly the way he'd done years ago. The sound of his voice thrilled her. His touch warmed her to the center of her soul. When he kissed her, she felt herself longing to give her heart to him over and over again.

"Good luck," he whispered before he kissed her. "And remember, I'll be here. Try to stay on the shore."

Clutching the boat-rental logbook to her chest, Tess stood on the rocks and watched Reed shove the small craft between two huge boulders that jutted up out of the water near the shore at the bay's north end, before he disappeared into the rocks himself to wait for the boat, whose lights Tess could already see approaching from the south.

Standing there waiting, the only sound Tess could hear was the beating of her own heart. The moon had disappeared again and the dark seemed to close around her, endless, ominous and foreboding. The pier jutted into what seemed like an endless black chasm. *The water is very deep,* Paolo had warned. A violent shudder shook her from within, and she held her breath and waited.

As THE BOAT drew near, Tess was struck first by its size. She hadn't really known what to expect, but the wide, flat-bottomed pontoon boat wasn't at all what she'd imagined. It looked more like a houseboat, the kind she'd seen on reservoirs back home. The vessel seemed a poor choice for a quick getaway.

The sound of scuffling feet and ropes being tossed onto the pier disturbed the quiet and sent shivers of dread tripping up and down Tess's spine. She strained her eyes, and saw two figures on the deck. A man and a woman. *Selena!* Tess's heart cried.

The couple made their way to the bow of the big square boat and stood looking toward the shore. From the glow of the lights behind her, Tess could make out her cousin's trim form. *Selena! Selena! You're alive*, her hearted rejoiced. *Oh, thank God you're alive!*

Tess's heart raced and she became fixated on her cousin's silhouette. The man stood slightly behind Selena and Tess imagined a gun at her cousin's back. No longer able to stand the silence or the suspense, Tess shouted, "Selena! I'm here. Over here!"

A spotlight hit her with the force of a physical blow, temporarily blinding her and her arm shot up reflexively to shield her eyes from the glare.

"Come aboard," the man shouted. "Walk down the pier."

Tess's heart sank. *Reed, did you hear him? Are you there?* Blindly she walked into the light toward the jutting concrete pier. *Reed! Oh, Reed, did you hear? I'm going aboard and I'm so frightened.*

"Raise your hands," the voice ordered, "so I can see what you have there."

"The journal. It's only Selena's notebook," she shouted and held it high over her head to prove she carried no weapon.

The spotlight proved to a blessing and a curse. It illuminated the narrow concrete pier, enabling Tess to see where she was walking, but every time she tried to look up at the boat, the light blinded her.

Keeping her head down, she fought to keep her balance on the wet, slippery pier. The waves thudded against the big boat in a taunting, rhythmic cadence as she moved closer. Despite the chilly breeze, she could feel a trickle of sweat scoot down her spine and when she glanced down at the dark swirling water she knew she'd made a mistake.

Momentarily, she lost her balance, and one leg plunged into the dark water, but she caught herself before she fell. Another five feet and she was facing a rope ladder. "Come aboard," the male voice ordered again.

Tess's hands were stiff with fear as she climbed the ladder and pulled herself up onto the wide deck. Mercifully, the spotlight was doused, but now she was blinded by the darkness. The logbook was jerked from her hands and a pair of rough hands trapped her wrists behind her in metal cuffs, while another pair of hands secured a thick, heavy cloth over her eyes.

"It's a fake!" someone shouted, and the rough hands shoved her and she fell helplessly onto the hard wooden deck.

"Selena!" she screamed. "Selena, it's Tess!" Her screams seared her throat. "Selena—" But before she could utter another word, she was gagged and pulled roughly to her feet and shoved down onto a wooden bench.

For a moment she could only sit in trembling helplessness, feeling wave after wave of shock washing over her. Before today no one had ever touched her in anger. The assaults to her body were taking a physical and emotional toll. A nagging voice told her she was weak and helpless and with the voice came panic.

But just as quickly her panic waned, as she reminded herself that she hadn't come all this way, survived all she'd survived just to give up now. Selena was depending on her. And even though Reed would try to help her, he'd warned her that once she was taken aboard the boat, a rescue would be difficult. Murmuring voices and shuffling sounds drew Tess's attention out of her own darkness.

She thought she heard a woman's voice and her heart ached. *Selena. Oh, Selena, I'm sorry!*

When she heard a man's voice suggest that they dispose of "the cousin" once they were underway, her terror redoubled. *Think, Tess!* she commanded herself. *Think! There has to be a way out!*

But when the pair of rough hands grabbed her again, she didn't have time to think. She could only react. And react she did, with her feet, kicking as hard as she could and as fast as she could. Kicking, kicking, viciously, wildly.

She rolled off the bench and onto her back and continued kicking and flailing her feet in the air. When she felt her foot make contact with something warm and soft, the gasp that followed told her it could have been a stomach. A heady sense of triumph filled her, rejuvenating her and giving her the strength she needed to continue her struggle.

When the hands came at her again, she rolled across the deck, scraping her head on something rough that snagged the blindfold and tilted it askew over one eye. She saw a movement to her left and rolled. When her tormentor came after her again, she kicked and rolled with all the strength she possessed and suddenly the blindfold fell away.

The man standing over her froze.

Tess blinked, and when her eyes adjusted to the light, what she saw shocked her speechless.

Chapter Sixteen

Selena's hair, which had been soft ash blond on Tuesday, had been dyed an almost blue-black. Gone were the springy curls, and the short boyish cap that replaced it clung to Selena's head and waved softly around her face.

"Hello, Tess." When she spoke Tess winced. The tall, tanned, fair-haired young man who seemed vaguely, naggingly familiar continued to hover over Tess, looking more confused and worried than ominous.

"Back off, Tony," Selena ordered. "It's too late. She's seen us."

The young man moved to the port side of the wide deck and picked up a rifle. Tess's breath caught as the very real possibility of her own death loomed before her startled and disbelieving eyes. He kept the rifle trained on her as Selena bent and jerked the gag from Tess's mouth and, grabbing her elbow, helped her up to sit on the narrow bench from which she'd fallen.

Tess's gaze flicked between her cousin and the man with the rifle. Something about his face triggered a memory and suddenly she remembered him as the waiter from the first day at West Palm. No wonder she had not been able to find him after Selena had left their table.

He muttered something to Selena before handing her the rifle. Oh, God! Something was so terribly, terribly wrong.

In a moment the lights went out and the deck was drenched in darkness except for a small gas lantern that left her and Selena encircled in a pool of soft light. "I was afraid you might not come, that we had frightened you too badly," Selena said.

Tess opened her mouth to speak, but the shock rippling through her had stolen her voice.

"Try to understand." Selena's voice was as steady as the weapon she clutched in her hand. "I had no choice."

Still stunned speechless and hopelessly confused, Tess saw Selena swallow a burst of emotion before she said, "I wanted to tell you, Tess. I tried to think of some other way. But they were after me. And then I heard they'd killed Andy Dianetti...."

"Morrell?" Tess supplied, almost without realizing she'd spoken.

Selena nodded. "Eddie Morrell will stop at nothing. He's ruthless, vengeful. I had to get away from him." Selena's eyes were shining and her voice shook.

"I wasn't just his bookkeeper, Tess. I was his lover. For three years. But soon there were other women. And then when I met Tony and found out all the things Eddie was into—the drugs and all the rest of it—well, I had to get away. Try to understand. I never meant for you to be hurt. Don't you see?"

Tess didn't see anything but a tangle of ugly deception. "I...I thought they'd kill you. I was so afraid I'd never see you again. And that man, Paolo, he terrorized me! Was that all your doing? Did you send that madman after me, Selena?" Even as she made the accusation, her mind refused to believe her cousin could have done such a horrible thing.

Selena's expression was one of heartfelt regret. "He was only supposed to frighten you, to make you believe that the threat to me was real. Just as we had to make you believe what was happening here tonight was real."

Bitterness rose like bile inside her. "Well, you made me a believer, all right! Damn it, Selena, how could you?" She'd never felt so betrayed, so used. Even when she'd believed Reed McKenna had betrayed her with her own sister.

"Tess, I'm sorry," Selena began, "but please, please try to understand. I—I had no choice."

Tess struggled to her feet and braced herself against the side of the boat, shaking her head and trembling all over as endless waves of fresh hurt mingled with grief washed over her. "I don't want to understand!"

she blurted. "Selena, I was nearly killed! And a man *was* killed in an explosion that was meant for me." Her voice was hoarse with the emotion clogging it.

"Explosion?"

"Come on, Selena. It's a little late to pretend innocence."

Something about the fear in Selena's eyes seemed real. "Tess, please. You have to listen. It isn't what you think. I had to make you believe I was in real danger, that my abductors had killed me. It was the only way."

Tony emerged from the darkened galley and took the rifle from Selena's hand. Tess's eyes darted from the weapon to her cousin's face. Selena's eyes were pleading. "We can't let you go, Tess. You know that, don't you?"

Reed! Tess's mind screamed. *Please, Reed! Help me!*

"Come below," Selena said quietly as though she were talking to a child. "Please, Tess. We've got to get underway. I'll explain everything. But now we have to get out of this bay before someone sees us."

Tess stared, still disbelieving, at the man with the rifle and this strange woman with the short black hair who was her cousin. Her mouth had gone almost too dry to speak. The pain that Selena had inflicted felt like a thousand needles in her heart, and looking into the pair of blue eyes so much like her own only made the pain worse.

"Please," Selena urged, reaching for Tess's arm and closing cold fingers around it. At her touch Tess jerked away, and out of the corner of her eyes she saw the rifle shift.

The look on Tony's face was nearly as desperate as Selena's. *They'll kill me,* she thought with stark amazement. *They're frightened. Desperate.* In her mind a dark whirlpool of fear threatened to spin her out of control. Unconsciously she began to edge toward the ladder, hoping that if somehow she could just get to it, she could find a means of escape.

"Tess, please," Selena said. "You must cooperate. I really don't want to hurt you."

"Then take these damn handcuffs off," Tess demanded with a strength she didn't know she possessed.

Tony glanced at Selena and she nodded. After handing her the rifle, he moved around behind Tess and unlocked the steel cuffs. The feeling rushed into Tess's hands like a jolt of electricity.

"Why couldn't you just leave Morrell, go to the authorities and strike a deal?" Tess asked, partly because she wanted to know, but mostly to buy precious time.

"Nobody just *leaves* Edward Morrell." Selena's voice was bitter. "That's why I thought if I could convince you I'd been abducted and murdered, then you'd convince everyone else. He'd have to believe it, too."

Tess shook her head.

"And there were other...considerations," Selena's voice cracked. "Other ties, things you know nothing about."

"Selena," Tess began, scrambling for the right words with which to reason with her cousin. "None of it matters anymore. Whatever you did, whatever trouble you're in, I would have helped you work it out. I'll still try. But you must come with me now. I promise, I'll do everything I can to help. But to go to this extreme to bring me out here and...hold me at gunpoint..." Tess realized she was on the verge of tears.

"We set it up so that when the time came, there wouldn't be any doubt." An ominous note had crept into Selena's voice.

"Selena, I'm getting off this boat," Tess said, her voice steadier and more resolved than she felt.

"Don't try it, Tess," Selena warned. Her voice was unrecognizably hard and her eyes shone with the desperation that had pushed her to this terrible extreme. "I don't know if I can kill my own cousin, but I can't let you go. We've come too far and there's too much at risk. And believe me, Tony *will* kill you if he has to." She made the declaration almost proudly. "He'd do anything to protect me, to protect our future together."

This was a nightmare, Tess told herself, a nightmare from which she prayed she'd soon awaken. "But why would you think you need protecting from me?"

Tess begged to know. "I would never hurt you, Selena! I only want to help."

"And you could have. This boat is rigged with explosives. Tony would have taken you ashore and we would have put out to sea. When we were far enough so that we could safely escape in the smaller boat we towed with us, we would have detonated the charge."

Tess shuddered. "My god, Selena, you're crazy!"

"Maybe. But now, thanks to you, our plans have had to change. For now, we'll have to take you with us."

At first Tess thought she only imagined the shadow moving behind Tony, but when she looked again and saw an arm snake out and grab the gun, sudden and utter relief flooded her.

"Get back. Both of you." Reed commanded, motioning Tony and Selena into the light.

Tess stood leaning against the railing where the ladder hung below. Her body had gone so weak that her legs wouldn't carry her to him. But her eyes met his and she knew he'd felt her touch.

"There is a coil of rope behind you, Tess. Pick it up and toss it to your cousin." His voice was low and firm and Tess clung to his reassuring control like a life preserver in a storm-tossed sea.

"Tie him, Selena," Reed instructed.

Tears streamed down Selena's cheeks as she bound Tony's hands behind him. "Please," she cried. "Please! You don't know what you're doing. Tess, you have to listen. It isn't just for me . . . it's for my baby!'' Selena dissolved in tears, while Tess could only stand staring, trying to absorb this latest blow.

"Your baby?" Tess gasped. "Selena?"

"She's not his!" Selena screamed defiantly, like some sort of jungle cat caught in a snare. "She belongs to Tony and me, and Eddie knows it. He only wants to take her away from me to punish me. Oh, Tess, please! Please, you have to let me go. I've got to find my baby." Selena fell into Tess's arms, her wracking sobs wrenching Tess's heart.

"Selena, please, please, tell me where is this baby?" Tess asked, her voice shaking.

"The county took her," she sobbed. "The judge ordered her into a foster home until after the trial. They wouldn't even let me see her. But I can't stand it!" She cried, her voice ragged. "Don't you understand? She's my baby!"

Tony's voice was trembling when he explained, "We paid fifty thousand dollars to a professional to snatch her and bring her to us here on the island. But when we arrived in Grand Cayman we discovered she'd been moved out of the home where they'd been keeping her."

"She's gone," Selena sobbed. "But if it's the last thing I ever do, I'll find her. I'll get her back. So help me, if I have to kill Eddie Morrell with my own hands."

Tony's eyes reached out to Selena with such love that Tess's heart went out to both of them. The desire to rescue her child from the far-reaching control of Edward Morrell had pushed Selena into this desperate and dangerous situation. Somehow, some way, Tess vowed to help her find a way out, a way to be reunited with her child—the little cousin Tess hadn't even known existed.

Reed's eyes held hers and something like regret flickered in their shadowy depths before he pulled something out of his pocket and handed it to Selena. It was a picture. "Crissy is in Grand Cayman," he said evenly. "She's all right."

The expression of shock that registered on Selena's face matched the frozen feeling in Tess's heart.

"But, how? Why?" Selena stammered. "I—I don't understand. How did you—"

"You would have used that baby," Tess gasped. "Used that little child to bring her mother in and collect your reward."

Reed's face had become a rigid mask.

"You son of a—" Tess's accusation was lost when a force around her throat sent an explosion of light sparking before her eyes.

"Drop the gun, McKenna." Through the pain and the confusion, Tess recognized the male voice coming from the ladder and the darkness behind her. The hard steel jabbing into her back told her she was in the arms of a cold-blooded killer.

"Nick!" Selena gasped.

"Hello, Selena," Talbot said calmly, his hold around Tess's throat unrelenting as he swung one leg and then another onto the boat. "I think you forgot something in your little plan, like the money Morrell owes me that you were to have transferred into one of our friendly Cayman banks. Somehow a deposit seems to be missing," he growled as he tossed Selena's journal at her feet. "But that measly sum doesn't matter now, because when Eddie finds out I've made sure you can't ever testify against him, and that you and your new lover are at the bottom of the bay, he'll pay me twice what you cheated me out of."

The gun shoved against Tess's temple dug into her flesh, and she felt fear like an icy hand at her throat.

Reed's expression was one of murderous rage. His jaw was clenching and unclenching like a machine.

With all the mental powers she possessed, Tess tried to telegraph her intent to him a split second before she acted. When her elbow jammed into Talbot's ribs, his hold on her loosened just enough for her to fall away from him.

The gasoline lantern was airborne before Tess saw Reed grab and throw it. Talbot swore and raised an arm to block the flaming missile and when he did, Reed lunged at him.

Tess rolled out of his way, just as Reed's shoulder made contact with Talbot's midsection. The breath went out of Talbot with a grunt and the gun went flying. It hit the deck and discharged, and Selena screamed. Tess's eyes locked on the rifle and she dove for it and came up shouting, "Stop! Everyone freeze!"

Reed grabbed Talbot by the collar and tried to haul him to his feet, but the weight of the big man sagged and above his pale blue eyes an ugly hole gaped where his own gun had sent a bullet.

Talbot's last expression seemed to be saying "So this is what it's like to die."

Chapter Seventeen

The farewell on the beach later that night was brief
and somber. Crissy clung a moment to Gertie and Jake
before she lunged into her mother's arms. Selena
seemed unable to stop crying as she covered her child's
face with kisses.

Tony hugged his daughter before he shoved the
small boat out into the water and cranked the outboard motor to life.

"Thank you both," Selena said, reaching for Gertie's hand and smiling at Jake. "I know you took good
care of my baby. I'll tell her all about you both some-
day."

Selena turned to Reed, the tears brimming in her
eyes. "How can I ever thank you?"

He shrugged, clearly embarrassed by her deep grat-
itude. "Take care of our little girl," was all he could
manage in a husky voice that caused Tess's heart to
contract.

"I hope my journal is enough to put Eddie behind bars for a long, long time."

Reed smiled. "I guess it will just have to be."

"Oh, Tess," Selena blurted, finally turning to her. "I'm sorry for what I put you through. You've been a good friend. Can you ever forgive me?"

"It's already forgotten. I love you, Selena. Take care. Have a good life." She wrapped her arms around what was left of her family, the family that would no longer exist once Selena and Crissy stepped into the boat and headed out for their new life with Tony and his family on the small island of Cayman Brac.

Crissy's incessant wiggling interrupted their embrace. "Goodbye, little one," Tess murmured, and planted a kiss on a cold, chubby cheek.

Gertie stood beside Jake, sniffing as the four of them watched the small boat moving steadily away from the shore. When the pale running light could no longer be seen, Reed turned to Tess and said, "Ready?"

She nodded and looked back out over the shimmering sea where the flames had been when Tony and Reed had taken the pontoon boat almost four miles out before they'd abandoned it.

The hours Selena and Tess had spent on the side of the hill in the safety of the cave waiting for the men to return had been a precious gift of time together that neither of them would ever forget.

When the men had finally rejoined them, Tony had activated the radio-controlled detonator and the four of them had watched from the hillside, speechless, mesmerized as the big boat went up in a ball of flame and smoke. It was all over quickly, the sea moving in to swallow the remnants of Nick Talbot's last trip to Grand Cayman.

"Well, so long, Tess," Gertie said, bringing Tess back to the present. "And don't forget to come by our place when you get back to Colorado."

Jake smiled as he shook both Tess's and Reed's hands. "See you back home, son," he said, holding Reed's eyes for a long, meaningful moment.

After Gertie and Jake left them alone on the beach, Reed and Tess stood together staring out at the sea.

"Do you think they'll make it?" Tess said finally.

"If they stick together, they will."

"The love between them was obvious, wasn't it?"

Reed nodded. "Crissy is a lucky little girl. Not every kid gets to grow up on an island."

"It's not Crissy anymore, remember?" During their last hours together, Selena had told Tess she'd secured new identity papers for all of them.

"It's Meredith," she reminded Reed softly, amazed she'd been able to speak around the catch in her throat.

He tightened his grip around her shoulders and together they started walking toward the beach house.

"I spoke to my contact in Washington when I went back for Gertie, Jake and the baby. He took the death of their key witness pretty hard, but he didn't seem surprised. It was difficult to let him believe Crissy had been killed in the blast, as well, but I couldn't see any way around it.

"By the way, they found evidence linking Talbot to the murder of Andy Dianetti. Charlie said they'd already issued a warrant to pick him up when he tried to reenter the country. When I told him Talbot had died when his own gun discharged and that I hadn't been able to get the body off the boat before it blew, Charlie didn't seem too disappointed. He bought the whole kidnapping story just the way Selena planned it."

Tess shivered. "Talbot planted the explosions at the bar that killed Davey, didn't he? The last thing he wanted was for me to find Selena before he did."

Reed nodded. "He was an explosives expert. If he'd been the one to rig the pontoon boat it would have gone up like a match when I tossed the oil lantern. We're lucky Tony was only an amateur."

"Do you think the journal will be enough to convict Morrell?"

"I hope so. Charlie was surprised by its existence and he can't wait to get his hands on it and turn it over to the I.R.S. Talbot must have paid someone to steal your purse that night in the restaurant. Ironic, isn't it, that he may be the one finally responsible for putting Morrell behind bars?"

They'd almost reached the beach house when she turned to him. "You gave Selena a precious gift. Her child was more important to her than even her own life."

He took her hand and pulled her down to sit beside him on the sand. He put his arm around her shoulders and stared east, where the sun was just beginning to cast a pink light along the horizon.

"I'll never know if I could have used that child to blackmail her into coming back." His fingers, entwined with hers, tightened as he spoke. "If I hadn't found you again, if you hadn't opened my heart again..." He swallowed before going on in a husky voice, "I guess I'll always wonder. It would have been the coward's way out."

"You're no coward, McKenna," she assured him.

"I wish I could believe that."

She kissed his cheek and saw that his eyes were glistening. Tears welled in her own eyes and her heart rose to her throat. "I believe it," she whispered. "And I believe in you, McKenna."

She went into his arms and he kissed her, softly, tenderly, so lovingly that she thought her heart might burst with all the love that filled it. When she opened her eyes, she gazed into the face of the man she knew would be her husband, her partner and her friend for the rest of her life. The trust between them had been tested and forged. Her love for him was deep, enduring and growing stronger every moment.

Reed kissed her again and then lifted his face to gaze into the eyes of the only woman he'd ever loved. When he saw her love shining back at him, his heart overflowed with hope, and he told himself that with her by his side, he could believe in anything, in new beginnings, in second chances, and even in himself.